Fanny-Maria Pittar

A protestant converted to catholicity by her bible and prayer book alone

Or, an account of the conversion of Mrs. Fanny Maria Pittar, written by herself

Fanny-Maria Pittar

A protestant converted to catholicity by her bible and prayer book alone
Or, an account of the conversion of Mrs. Fanny Maria Pittar, written by herself

ISBN/EAN: 9783741193156

Manufactured in Europe, USA, Canada, Australia, Japa

Cover: Foto ©Andreas Hilbeck / pixelio.de

Manufactured and distributed by brebook publishing software
(www.brebook.com)

Fanny-Maria Pittar

A protestant converted to catholicity by her bible and prayer book alone

A PROTESTANT CONVERTED TO CATHOLICITY

BY HER

BIBLE AND PRAYER BOOK ALONE.

A PROTESTANT

CONVERTED TO CATHOLICITY

BY HER

BIBLE AND PRAYER BOOK ALONE:

OR,

AN ACCOUNT OF THE CONVERSION OF

MRS. FANNY MARIA PITTAR.

WRITTEN BY HERSELF.

REVISED BY A

CATHOLIC PRIEST.

THIRD EDITION.

LONDON:
RICHARDSON AND SON;
DUBLIN; AND DERBY.
MDCCCLXVII.

PREFACE OF THE EDITOR.

It is now about twenty years since the following pages were given to the public. The writer—a lady still living in retirement, mostly on the continent—was educated as a member of the Church Established by Law, in this country. Her maiden name was Wareing. Having married, and her husband being obliged to reside in India, where she too had been, her temporary separation from him afforded her happy leisure for studying the business of her own salvation. How solicitous she was to arrive at the knowledge of the truth; and the manner in which she was led to it, can be clearly seen in her own simple narrative, which cannot weary the reader, it is so earnestly and faithfully recorded by herself.

Her object in giving the history of her conversion in a printed form, was twofold. The first, was to satisfy her family and friends, that every step she took in this question of questions, was in obedience to the inward impulse of her own conscience, directed by Divine Grace. The second was, that if this little book, so candidly written, should fall into the hands of persons perplexed, as she was, and having no authority to guide them higher than the Prayer-Book of the Church of England, and, as a matter of course, the Testament, which is in the hands of all Christians, and to which all lay equal claim, they may be encouraged by her example, not to rest contented until they find a living authority, speaking the whole truth of God, and inspired by His Spirit with power from above.

In speaking upon this subject with her, previous to the publication of her book: What struck her, she said, particularly, was, that in the Church of England, as well as in the Presbyterian Calvinism of Scotland, and in all the other sects throughout the United Kingdom, there was evident absence of an authority or a tribunal to decide questions of faith. She, moreover, perceived that the science of salvation was not like a human science.

Its teachers must have a special mission from God: " How can they preach unless they be sent ?" She saw clearly from her knowledge of the various religious systems around her, that in none of them was Faith made *objective*, or delivered, defined, and declared by unerring authority ; but, on the contrary, Faith was subjective ; and that the right of Private Judgment had left each one to choose between the various doctrines of belief, rejecting or adopting for himself, as he thought proper. This great and fallacious principle of the " Reformation," has kept, and will keep all who have strayed from the Church, or who have been brought up outside of her pale, in a state of doubt, to be "tossed to and fro by 'every wind of doctrine."

Moreover, she declared she could not find the Church of Christ as it should be —judging from the Testament—exemplified in any of the communions or religious bodies around her. None of them taught " all truth." The Church of Christ must be one. It must be also universal. These notes her Testament showed her : " One fold, one shepherd." "Go teach all nations." This she saw must be the office of the One Church, By what communion of Christians is this universal teaching fulfilled? was a question she asked herself continually. Without going to Apostolic succession and sanctity of its members, she saw at least the necessity of Unity and Catholicity. These facts forcibly struck her. She could only find the features of the Church as defined by the Scriptures, reflected from the great body of Christians in communion with the See of Rome—the unvarying centre of Christendom.

As regards the Prayer-Book of the Church of England, I may here remark, as she did, that its Liturgy is in great part Catholic, having been taken from the Missal, or Mass-Book of the Universal Church, whilst upon the Thirty-nine Articles there is the unmistakable stamp of Protestantism. The articles are partly Lutheran and partly Calvinistic. In order to please these two great sections of Protestantism, which were rival powers for a long time contending for the supremacy in the state, it was necessary to frame, or define, articles of belief, that might suit

both, if not unite them. Hence, we find
that neither of them is Lutheran, pro-
perly so called. The one rejoicing in
the name of Presbyterianism, and being
the State Church of Scotland, has its
independent confession of faith, the Westminster Confession. It is not pure Calvinism. The other, in order, as above
stated, to please all, professes half Calvinism. Although it retained a form of
government similar to the old Church of
the country, and although its public worship was so framed as to please the people, having many of the features of the
ancient Liturgy? yet the Latitudinarian
principle became so thoroughly interwoven
with its first principles, a wide door for
dissent was opened, and by-and-bye the
right of Private Judgment, rising like a
flood, swept over all barriers, and engen-
dered the various sects that have since
rent society asunder, each claiming for
itself the doctrine of Exclusive Salvation.

In the Appendix to this book there will
be more upon this subject.

In conclusion, we may briefly enumerate
the errors that led away from the Church
those who are not contented with the

faith of Christendom in these islands. The right of Private Judgment was claimed by all sects, thus contradicting the ordinary rule, "faith comes by hearing." "Justification by faith alone," or the Solifidian doctrine, overthrew the sanctity of morals. The doctrine of election of grace and predestination took away free will in the work of salvation. I stop here lest I should weary the reader, and will again refer him to the Appendix. One principle, however, we beg to notify as characteristic of nearly all was this, that conscious their work was not of God, but of man's creation, they fled to the state or civil power for protection, and in order to this they resigned their spiritual power or authority into the hands of the civil magistrate, who, by accepting such new power, bound himself in some sort to protect it. This is what is called Erastianism, or the civil power assuming to be the head of the Church, as we see exemplified in nearly all the countries of Europe, where the rights and privileges of the Holy See have been disowned, and where the children have revolted against the obedience claimed by our holy mother the Church, in every age and in every place wheresoever the empire of Christ extended.

The sandy foundation whereon each sect establishes its power is Private Judgment, not the Rock of the Church. The Bible, interpreted according to this principle, causes the strange diversion of doctrine, the multitude of opinions which contain much of truth as well as of error, thus bewildering the minds of the people. Having rejected the authority of the Church, and quitted her pale, it was feasible, at least, they should keep her book, which, being interpreted, according to the judgment of the various teachers, has been the fertile source of endless errors; and hence St. Jerome declares, "the Bible misinterpreted has been the source of all heresy."

DEDICATION.

TO THE RIGHT REV. DR. GILLIS, BISHOP OF
LIMYRA, COADJUTOR VICAR APOSTOLIC OF
THE EASTERN DISTRICT OF SCOTLAND.

MY DEAR LORD—From the circumstance
of your having admitted me into the Catholic
Church, and having been a powerful instrument in leading me into truth, I am induced
to address to your Lordship the following brief
account of my conversion, as a little offering of
gratitude—little indeed, nevertheless, watered
with many tears, and recommended to God by
many prayers. May I hope it will not only be
acceptable to yourself, but also prove salutary
to others.

You know, my dear Lord, the boon I have
received—you know something of the burstings of my overjoyed soul, but you cannot
know, (having inherited your holy faith,) the
rapture, the bliss of being converted, and newly
adopted to this life-giving truth, when the
understanding is ripe, and capable in some
degree of appreciating the treasure. St. Mary

Magdalen could, perhaps, describe it, or the Lepers who felt the loathsome disease depart, as health came back; but for me, my Lord, there is no relief but to sit down and pen this little account, not so much with the idea of making it public, as simply to relieve myself, in the hope of its one day becoming a medium of addressing those I love best upon the subject, and whose applications to me have been made without number, to be informed of the reasons that led to my conversion.

To neglect to reply to these inquiries I dare not, and yet, a life would be too short to answer them all as I would wish. The account, however, put in this form, will be a ready reply to all; and oh! my Lord, feeble as the effort is, you who know the value of even one soul, and the numbers who, like myself, are inquiring for truth, from a source, whence they never can get it, will not chide me for simply telling the truth, although by so doing, I am very well aware of the pain I must inflict on your charitable heart, by the unavoidable reference to some characters therein alluded to. Yes, I know you will be distressed at it, but be assured, my Lord, we are mutual sufferers on that point, for I am truly distressed at it myself. But when, I would ask your Lordship, is the acceptable

offering without sacrifice? Most truly I
must calculate on considerable sacrifice, but
when such thoughts depress me, I think
of my former danger, and of my narrow
escape. Only think, my Lord, had these
well-meaning but deceived gentlemen, only
dealt a little more cautiously, a little
more reasonably with me, I might have
been lost to truth for ever. But blessed be
God, their dealings with me ended all my
ramblings in the dark. It might not be so,
however, with others. Shall I, therefore, to
spare these poor deluded men, towards whom I
feel nothing but gratitude, neglect to warn
others?

My Lord, believe me, I have mourned over
the distance between us, which prevented me
from having your particular advice upon this
matter; but I have thought it well over, and
every day I neglect to " throw in my mite,"
by telling how I was led to truth, I expect to
be judged, at every step I take. Had I had
you near me to correct and revise, truly this
little work would have been a' different affair;
but perhaps, my Lord, it is better as it is. I
am nobody, and consequently there is nobody
to blame. You could not have touched it,
without your pen telling upon itself, whereas it
is now ungarnished truth, and when that will
fail to reach the heart, it can be set down as

beneath notice, which advantage it would not have possessed, had you meddled with it at all. Accept, therefore, my dear Lord, this little tribute from a heart overflowing with gratitude, both to God, as the first great cause, and also to yourself, and the other individuals, whom He used as instruments to deliver me from doubt and inconsistency, and safely lodge me in His own most glorious Church, "without spot or wrinkle, or any such thing," where truth speaks for itself, and the peace of her children knows no uneasiness.

Allow me, therefore, to implore your Lordship's prayers and blessings upon this narrative, and believe me in all sincerity your Lordship's truly indebted, and thankful child in Christ,

FANNY MARIA PITTAR.

April, 1845.

PREFACE.

———

WITH the truest sincerity, humility, and natural timidity, I take up my pen to trace, for the first time in my life, lines that are to meet the public eye. I have done my best to argue myself out of such a project—I have felt and urged upon myself my utter inability for the task. I have left no method untried, by which I might frighten myself out of it. My efforts are in vain. I feel urged on by an influence I have no power to control, and I feel utterly regardless of the personal contempt and scorn, I may most justly expose myself to, from my attempt. The effort must be made, let the result be what it may; not that I am regardless of consequences, when I can, and ought to avoid them; but my present effort I feel to be of such vast importance, if I only succeed, so as to bear a message to *one* dear soul, that all nice feelings, all fears of personal inability, all doubts as to the results it may produce, *all, and everything,* are to be disregarded and cast aside.

At once, therefore, I go to my task, keeping

2

in mind, as a stimulant, those most comforting
words to me, who feel so completely nothing:
—" The foolish things of the world hath God
chosen, that He may confound the wise ; and
the weak things of the world hath God chosen
that He may confound the strong. And the
base things of the world, and the things that
are contemptible hath God chosen, and things
that are not, that He might bring to nought
things that are." It may not be forbidden me
here to hope, that He will not refuse me His
aid, in an effort that has nothing to recom-
mend it, but as far as it is intended for His
greater glory, and the advancement of His
truth. Nor will it have aught to boast of,
save the simplicity, truth, and sincerity, which
will dictate every line. With the learned and
great I have nothing to do, but I do feel I
have a message to every humble and sincere
Protestant, who values the salvation of his
precious and immortal soul, and that message,
to the best of my ability, I will deliver. It is
simply this—I feel, that to many I owe a
reason for having, in the short space of one
month, abjured the faith in which I was
reared and lived ; and lived, not as many do,
with only the name of Christianity, and without any vital principle within ; but upon the
testimony of others, which I have " in black
and white," I am able to say, I was a sincere

Protestant, believing I possessed the truth of God, or, at least, that I was in the Church, where it was to be found, having sought it earnestly and with many tears, caring for nothing else in comparison, for at least the last twelve years of my life. Persevering in the search of truth, by the grace of God, I suddenly find it lies, not where I had formerly conceived, but in a Church, which I had been taught from my cradle to believe as the sink of all iniquity, the concentration of all error and untruth—even in this Church I discover that the *infallible truth of God lies*—that truth which *declares itself* to be of God, and leaves the soul that has been searching for it so long and so earnestly, though not for a moment conceiving where it was to be found, so ravished with its *beauty* and its *security*, as to be almost unfit to declare it to others, lest it should be said, as was of those of old, when influenced by Divine power—" Those men are full of new wine !"

The grace being given, I entered this faith, which I had sought so long with my whole heart, and in embracing it, I enjoy a peace I never knew before, a certainty I had in vain striven to attain as a Protestant, and daily and hourly means of serving God, which no Protestant need hope for, since his Church thinks one day out of seven sufficient to devote

to God, or at least to go to the trouble of
public service to Him.   Having all this, I feel
a burning desire to tell it to all—to every one,
and they can judge for themselves from the
reasons I shall give, whether or not they be
sufficient for the change?

To each and every beloved member of my
own family, I address myself in particular, as
also to each individual of that Protestant circle,
to which, but a short time since, I belonged ;
yes, and even to every Protestant, whose eye
may fall on these lines, and who is, as I was,
serving God to the best of his ability, according to the rule of faith inherited from his
parents, in sincerity desiring to serve God as
He requires, even to the sacrifice of all selfish
and worldly interest—to such, and for their
sakes only do I pen these lines.

To many it may be my privilege to communicate, in person, the reasons of this great
change, but alas! to those who are most
endeared, and most closely connected, I fear
not.   The beloved child once honoured with
her parents' unlimited confidence and love,
has by this act forfeited all claim to either ; she,
whose word and example were once upheld,
must now bear to be told she is incapable of
judging aright on any subject.   Well, be it so
—all this and ten times more I can and will
bear from such dear ones, who, after all, are

only pronouncing the very words I should myself have uttered hitherto. But if the privilege of explaining to these precious souls the reasons of my change be denied me, it surely behoves me to try, and put them in a form, by which I may hope sooner or later to acquaint them of these reasons. God deals differently with different people, and why I have become a Catholic may not be why another would do so. The following simple detail is therefore penned only for those who may be circumstanced as I myself was, without either learning, talent, or any uncommon share of *brains*, (for had any of these been necessary to "ferret" out truth from Catholicity, I should never have been a Catholic,) but with only a sufficient quantity of humility to feel it possible I might be wrong, and a very earnest desire to be right, trusting to the truth of God's promise, that those who seek shall find, and feeling sure that I should be right sooner or later, if I persevered to seek. I did so, and having sought, I am, at last, able to say I have found, yes, all that any one could desire—all that my soul required ! Now, as I know there are numbers, who care for nothing compared to the salvation of their souls, and who feel the value of that rule of faith, which teaches them they are to search for truth, (thereby implying the possibility, that they may not already possess it,) and who therefore, need only be told what truth is, that they may instantly embrace it, to them my heart yearns, and for them I will make the effort of putting my reasons on paper. But should these lines meet the eye of any learned Protestant, who detects in them defects of style or composition, let him cast them aside, as utterly unworthy of his criticism, and spare them, remembering they come only from a woman, and were never meant to display either talent or learning, but only to affect the heart, in as far as they have truth to support them.

CONVERTED TO CATHOLICITY ·

———

Early in February, 1842, under the good
Providence of God, I left Dublin, an humble,
but zealous Protestant, to make a visit to a
lady, a friend of mine in Edinburgh, (my husband being in India.) She and I had met in
India, where we held the same faith, but by
the power of Him, who willeth and no man
can hinder it, she was converted to the Catholic
faith, between our parting in India, the previous
December, and our meeting in Edinburgh.
However, that had nothing to do with our
friendship, except as it might make her love
me better. I had got a slight inkling of her
change, previous to my going to her, though
not certain information ; however, sufficient to
arm myself with all the weapons I could collect
from our Protestant armoury—books, pronounced to be by a clerical friend, " the cream"
of argument against Catholicity, together with

personal instructions on different points. Thus
assisted, I started, earnestly imploring I might
be made the humble instrument of leading my
friend *back to truth*, little thinking the prayer I
offered so earnestly for another's benefit, would
be so graciously returned into my own soul.
A very short time after my arrival, I endured
the heart-sickening every Protestant feels on
hearing, for a certainty, that one of their own
faith had been converted to Catholicity. It
imparts a sorrow, that is as much without
hope, as that which one feels for the dead, at
least, as regards the hope of seeing them back
again where they were before. However, I
was not going to yield to despair, until I had
first exhausted the ammunition I had in store.
Besides the books I had bought, I conceived I
myself understood the doctrine of Catholicity,
at least, I knew I had heard enough of it to
be perfectly satisfied it was utterly horrible,
and that to embrace it, one must have entirely
lost every proper feeling of what was just and
good. Besides, coming from a Catholic city,
as Dublin might almost be called, I felt I could
assert with boldness all the abominations of
this faith; not that I had ever personally ex-
perienced or witnessed any of its baneful results,
or derived my Catholic knowledge from Catholics—no, but every one agreed that nothing
could be more horrible than the Catholic faith

was, and I thought so too. Moreover, I had read dreadful things of it, and I thought, of course, what I read *in print* was true, *especially as the author was some celebrated Protestant*, and so, I am certain, think the great majority of Protestants everywhere. But more just and liberal light has since dawned upon me, as, I pray God, it may ere long on many, who need but the veil taken from their eyes, the prejudices of their early faith removed, the hint given, that the Catholic Church is the true Church of Christ, and the means of learning what the Catholic faith *really is*, presented to them. This done, the speediest means of bringing these persons into this Church without delay, is just to place in their hands for candid examination their Bible and Prayer Book, and, if you please, a few of what my friend termed the *cream of arguments against Catholicity.* The coolness with which Protestants assert what Catholics believe, the absurdities they put into their mouths, and the splendid argument they get up, and triumphantly get through against a phantom that never existed—a creature of their own creating, strike, at once, an intellect in search of truth, and do more to establish upon " the rock of ages" a wavering mind, than all the talents ever heaped upon man could accomplish.

But to continue:—After giving a fortnight or

so, to seeing the " lions" of the place, I thought
of the mission I had come upon, and, with
anxiety, looked for an opportunity to address
my friend upon the subject of the change she
had made in her religion. One by one, I enu-
merated to her the horrible doctrines of the
Church of Rome. To each one I received
answer, that such and such was not Catholic
doctrine at all. This was a course I never expected the affair to take, and for which I was
quite unprepared. I had thought she would
have tried to defend this and that doctrine, but,
plumply to tell me all I said and conceived to
be Catholic doctrine was utterly false, startled
me not a little. However, although I did feel
much puzzled, I took good care she should not
see I was so. I certainly did feel either, that
she was not yet initiated into what really was
Catholic doctrine, or else that I had been
grossly deceived, from my very cradle, upon
the subject.

Amongst the other " lions" of the city, I
was taken to hear and see the Rev. Mr. C——,
of the Episcopal Church. He was called a
great preacher, and certainly gave us a fine
sermon. Next in order was Mr. D——, of
the same establishment, noted for his great
piety and spirituality; then the Rev. Dr.
C—h, a Presbyterian minister of great renown;
and lastly, the Episcopalian Bishop. Descant-

ing on the merits of these preachers, all of whom I found my friend had heard, she timidly inquired whether I would go and hear a sermon in her church. Anxious to prove to her the stability of the faith I held, and which she had forsaken, and that it would be unshaken by anything a Catholic priest could say, I readily assented. Besides, I had visited Catholic churches on the Continent, and knew of my parents having conducted their children to them, as things worthy of notice when travelling; so that the idea of fear or hazarding my faith by so doing, never entered my head. The preacher, the Right Rev. Dr. Gillis, chose for his subject a topic, which, when he first announced it, filled my soul with a feeling of triumph. I thought I needed no better proof of the ungodliness of the Catholic Church. He commenced by calling the attention of his congregation to the Protestant Calendar, the Catholic Calendar, and the Infidel Calendar of France! He said, as the index of a book shewed what was contained therein, so a Calendar declared the feelings and habits of the nation or body to which it belonged. I shall for briefness' sake, merely notice a few of his remarks on the Protestant and Catholic Calendars, which he read out, and took for example the month he was then in—February.

PROTESTANT CALENDAR.	CATHOLIC CALENDAR.
1 Fisheries north of Tweed open	1 St. Ignatius
2 Partridge and Pheasant Shooting ends	2 Purification of the Blessed Virgin Mary
3 Sexagesima Sunday	3 St. Blase
4 Purification of the Blessed Virgin, or Candlemas	4 St. Andrew Corsini
5 Dr. Cullen died, 1790	5 St. Agatha
6 Dr Priestly died, 1804	6 St. Dorothy
7 Bishop Keith born, 1781	7 St. Ronald
8 Mary Queen of Scots beheaded. 1587	8 St. John of Matha
9 Dr. J Gregory died, 1733	9 St. Apollonia
10 Quinquagesima Sunday	10 St. Scholastica
11 Descartes died, 1615	11 St. Raymond of Penafort
12 Shrove Tuesday	12 St. Catherine
13 Ash Wednesday	13 St. Benedict
14 St. Valentine	14 St. Valentine
15 Tweed Net and Rod Fishery opens	15 St. Faustinus and Jovita
16 Melancthon born, 1497	16 St. Onessimus
17 1st Sunday in Lent	17 St. Fintan
18 Luther born	18 St. Simeon
19 Sun enters Pisces	19 St. Barras
20 Rev. Charles Wolf died, 1823	20 St. Tyrannio, &c.
21 James I. assassinated. 1437	21 St. Severianus
22 Adam Ferguson died	22 The Chair of St. Peter
23 Duke of Cambridge born	23 St. Serenus
24 2nd Sunday in Lent	24 St. Mathias
25 St. Mathias, Apostle	25 St. Tarasius
26 Sir T. Craig died	26 St. Alexander.

From thence he proved the Protestant nation had not their every day devoted to God, but thought that by heaping all their devotion upon a Sunday, they served God admirably. A few days certainly were devoted to the honour of some saint or holiday, but devoted to them only to condemn them. For, from

what authority or source could Protestants
acknowledge such things as saints' days?
They who hold no rule of faith but the Bible,
could not dream of a St. Valentine or a Shrove
Tuesday, or an Ash Wednesday therein. "Do
Protestants know," he inquired, "why or
whence they hold these days? No, they
either do not know, or knowing, they dare not
say, for it is from the Catholic Church they
received them, and to say so would proclaim
their inconsistency. For instance, let any
Protestant present, if such there be," (and
there was one to whom he was, at the command of heaven, bearing a message, though he
knew it not,) "let him go and ask his clergyman what the approaching Wednesday means,
(Ash Wednesday.) He will see it in his
prayer book, and in his calendar too, and the
day after he can, from the same source, send
Valentines, or commence fishing in the Tweed
with nets or rods ; but will he see anything of
it in his churches, or hear anything from his
ministers to tell him why the day is so called?
No, he will not, because they can only give
him *a Catholic reason.* On the contrary, *every
day* in the Catholic Church and calendar is
devoted to some holy recollection. The
Catholic Church, and it only, is open *every day*
for devotion, and every day provides for the
souls of the people 'daily bread,' a means of

offering the first of each day to their Creator,
and of sanctifying their secular employments.
The pure Sacrifice and clean Oblation, declared
by Malachy i. 11, as a thing which should be
offered daily, ' from the rising of the sun to
the going down of the same,' even for ever-
more, is daily offered from the *Altars* of the
Catholic Church, and it only." He said much,
very much more, that I am utterly incapable
of attempting to repeat, and much that I then
wished he had kept to himself, and most truly
did I regret that all he said was so much to
the purpose, and so convincing of this one
point, that the religion of the Catholic Church
taught and influenced men from Sunday morning to Saturday night. All this I heard with
very great astonishment, and all he said was
alarmingly and hatefully true. In fact, such
a powerful sermon I had never before heard,
and coming from a Catholic priest or bishop, it
made no matter which, I was utterly puzzled,
and when my friend inquired what I thought
of her preacher, I knew not what to say. I
wished from my soul that the man who could
so metamorphose what I thought a lie into
truth, had never been born, or else that I had
been born to know *that truth*, which I had
always conceived a lie. His subject, which
commenced so antichristian, as I thought,
closed with Christ as its beginning and its end,

its all in all.   I confess I was thoroughly bewildered.   The idea that perfect truth could
be in the Catholic Church, almost deprived me
of the power to proceed, and yet *I felt* the
preacher's words were true.   However, I had
no idea of allowing either to my friend or myself, that I was in any measure conquered.   It
was very true, he had had it all his own way
in the pulpit, and so far I was bound to credit
him right, till I had proved him wrong.   But I
would do as he desired, I would put the question he proposed to a clergyman, and I felt no
doubt his eloquence and apparent truth would
both vanish before the answer I should get.
For although, to my shame, I could not give a
satisfactory explanation of Ash Wednesday,
still I would go to one whose business and
delight I felt it would equally be, as a preacher
of the Protestant Church, to enlighten me.

Ash Wednesday soon came; I went to
hear Mr. ——, celebrated alike for learning
and piety, an Episcopalian, and altogether the
man for me. I listened, all anxiety, to his
sermon, hoping I should hear what would
enable me to silence my friend, without any
personal application being necessary, and to
prove to her she had made a mistake, or at
least her bishop had, in supposing our clergy
could not give a reason, and a good one too,
for everything in their Church. The sermon

commenced and ended, but not one word of,
or about "Ash Wednesday." What was I
to do? I was a total stranger to the preacher,
and still, I felt this was no time to stand upon
ceremony. It was a matter of importance to
me to have the question answered, for should
what the Catholic bishop said of the calendar
be true, (which, of course, I could not suppose
possible, and still I could not shake off the
impression it had left,) what he said on other
subjects might be so also, and then, alas, for
me! I approached the rev. gentleman as he
descended the pulpit stairs, apologised for
stopping him, but said I was a stranger in
Edinburgh, anxious to have a question answered which had been put to me by a
Catholic, viz.: *What was the exact meaning of
Ash Wednesday?* and that I was ashamed to
say I had not been able to give a proper answer. He took my hand with the greatest
kindness, and cheered me by the most friendly
reception, and said, looking me hard in the
face, "You are aware we Protestants have
nothing to do with *ashes*, or *candles*, or
CROSSES, or any such nonsense." Yes, sir, I
said, I know that. "Well," he continued,
"that being the case, *the day is more a name
than anything else*, and indeed it should not
be in the Prayer Book, no more than Christmas day, which ought to be called the *Nati-*

vity of our Lord. Such terms, *Christmas day,* and *Ash Wednesday,* and some others, were quite Catholic, and spoke for themselves being so, and indeed such things needed reforming before being placed in a reformed Prayer Book." At these words my heart sank : all the Catholic priest had said rushed into my mind, and a horrid thought crossed me, and forced itself upon me, *that perhaps my long-treasured faith was insecure!* When I could speak I said, But sir, am I to say what you have said to my friend? "No, no," said he, "*just* say, that ashes are typical of humility, and *therefore* the day is called Ash-Wednesday to remind us of the time it ushers in, in which we are to humble ourselves by prayer and *fasting.*" Fasting, sir! said I, almost choking with the feelings contending within me ; if I· say "fasting," my friend will naturally triumph over me again, for you know, sir, *we don't fast.* "That, my dear, is quite *another* subject, therefore, *say nothing* of fasting," (and looking at me very hard, and drawing me quite close to him,) "you know my child, there are *different meanings* that can be attached to that word, and besides you know many good Protestants do fast ; but as your mind does not seem *quite established,* I would advise you *not to use the word,* but merely say *to humble ourselves by prayer.*"

8

And is that the answer, sir? said I, scarcely able to articulate; upon which I raised my eyes, and at the same time they met his, which were anxiously resting upon me, and with much alarm in his look, he took hold of my two hands, and said, "May I urge upon you, a total stranger, the *ill effects of Catholic society.* Avoid it—do, for, believe me, you will get no good, whatever harm you may from it." We parted, my head full of confusion, my heart full of sadness. I tried to avoid the subject with my friend, but she was too anxious to impart to me some of the joy and peace she herself had, so she instantly required to be enlightened. I gave the words delivered to me, and to which she simply replied : "And do you think that satisfactory?" No, I said, I do not; and though at this, I dare not disclose to her, or allow myself for a moment to feel my faith was not founded upon a rock, still I inwardly felt a great desire to know really what the Catholic faith was, but I knew not how to go about it. I commenced, however, by making attacks upon the different points of her belief.

The first thing I enquired after, or rather insisted upon was, that the Pope was considered by all Catholics *individually infallible,* that he was called by Catholics "*God,*" and that every title given in Scripture to Christ was ascribed to him; this idea I got out of one of the books I had brought with me to convert my friend. To my astonishment she boldly declared such was not, *nor ever had been* a doctrine of the Catholic Church ; no more is he called or entitled God, than any nobleman would be when, addressed in Latin, he is styled "*Dominus :*" and so far from his being considered impeccable, he continually humbles himself by falling upon his knees to confess his sins to a poor monk, besides which he can never offer up the sacrifice of the Mass without making a public confession of his sins, in the same manner as the humblest priest, by reciting the "confiteor" in the commencement of the Mass.

The next point I asserted with great determination, because I remembered having read a *most convincing book founded upon the very fact* (Father Clement!) was, that to this hour the Church forbids the use of Scripture to the laity. Here again I was baffled, she assured me no such command or restriction was laid upon Catholics ; so far from it, proper translations of the Bible were, and are circulated by *order* of the Church, wherever people can be found capable of reading them ; besides, I knew her to have become, since her conversion to Catholicity, quite a Biblical scholar.

My next attempt was aimed at confession.

I exclaimed with horror at a doctrine so re-
pugnant to human nature, as that of confess-
ing one's sins to a priest, and then, to complete the matter, of supposing he had power,
after hearing, to pardon. This I knew was a
Catholic doctrine, and Catholic only; so I
anticipated a glorious triumph, as far as this
point went, and I was more successful than on
the two former subjects, at least I was not
told that what I was stating was false; but I
question whether my defeat was not more perfect. She alleged, that *confession* and *absolution* were not only Catholic doctrine *by Scripture warranted*, but also the professed doctrine of the Episcopal Church, to which I
belonged. For proof, she referred to the
Protestant Prayer Book, at the " Visitation
of the Sick," where it is enjoined upon the
minister, *to move the sick person to confess his
sins, and then to absolve him.* I opened my
prayer book, and found it *even so*, and I con-
fessed I was puzzled, because I felt certain,
if Christ had left power to His ministers to
forgive sins at the hour of death, they had the
same power at *any other time.* I also felt if
it were good to confess one's sins on the
death-bed to a priest, how much better and
infinitely more beneficial it must be to humble
oneself, when in health and strength, and
liable to sin every moment, than to postpone it

to a time which may never come. Besides the obligation which in health and strength must of necessity have a great power to check sin, brings much comfort to the soul, and powerfully assists to lead a godly life. But I really know not what to make of it all; I seemed to be but awaking out of a deep sleep, the past being like a dream compared to the reality dawning upon me.

I thought, however, I would make another attempt, which I did by mocking the idolatrous practice used in all ages of the Church, that of worshipping angels and the Blessed Virgin Mary, as God, and therefore taking from God's glory, besides the absurdity of supposing they could either hear our petitions, or grant them if they did. In answer to this I was informed that the Church had *at no time* sanctioned the worship of angels, or of the Blessed Virgin, *as God;* and that we know from Scripture they have the power to benefit and succour us, else why would Jacob (Gen. xlviii. 16,) call upon an angel to bless the sons of Joseph? Or why did Josue fall down to worship the angel? (Josue v. 14, 15.) Or why would our Saviour Himself have said, (Matt. xviii. 10) "See that you despise not one of these little ones, for *their* angels are always before the face of My Father in heaven?" A Catholic, therefore,

feels it not inconsistent to seek and implore
their aid and assistance.   Besides, Protestants
acknowledge the principle, but in practice deny
it, as may be seen in their Prayer. Book, in
the Collect to St. Michael.   More bewildered·
now than ever, I knew not what to think
either of what I heard or what I saw.   I felt
a strange misgiving that I was being deceived
by my informants, and still my eyes beheld
the words in the Bible; nor could I assign
any advantage it would give them to lead me
astray, for I could not suppose people of common sense could hope to increase their numbers and extend their faith, by concealing and
disguising the *real doctrine* they professed.
Besides, they did not seek me, they offered
no instruction, no interference, until it was
sought by me.   I am not ashamed to say
that by this time I felt desirous to inquire
of better authority than Protestants, what the
Catholic faith really was, as all I was now
hearing seemed as new to me, and as perfect,
as if it came straight from God.   So feeling
thus, I naturally determined to inquire of a
priest what the Catholic religion was, as I
considered such the only authority I could depend upon.

   Just at this critical moment, by the direction of Providence, an old friend, the Rev.
Mr. H. arrived in Edinburgh.   When I

inquired of him what brought him, he said really he did not know; that he came on his way from Dublin to London! Many may wonder where the interference of Providence appears in this; but I would ask such, is Edinburgh the usual way of going from Dublin to London? Besides which I have it in writing from him, that he came *only to see me*, although we had only parted in Dublin a very short time before, and when there, although we were very intimate, still weeks, nay months, often passed without our meeting, and neither of us were less happy on that account, as also this additional fact, that although he came to go to London, he did not do so, but returned to Dublin, without being able to assign any reason for not proceeding to London.

I now thought God had sent me one who would fight my battles for me, and although I expected he would have helped me differently, still it was not the less effectual. I therefore handed him over to my friend to prove to her she was all wrong, never supposing, for a moment, her arguments would stand before a clergyman. They had a good deal of conversation upon many points of controversy, but she, finding he had ways of leaving a subject when he was unable to defend it, (which I too could but perceive to be the case,) requested he would see a priest, who, she doubted not would be his match, and not let him turn from a subject just as he felt he was conquered. He very kindly said, Certainly, he would see a priest, if he was likely to do her any good by it, as he feared no man, with his Bible in his hand.

I felt this was a critical moment for me, for I determined, by his defence I would stand or fall, that is, if I saw he was able to give a reason, against the Catholic arguments, for the faith he professed, I would never think of Catholicity more, never yield my Protestant faith; but if he failed, I held myself bound to search for that faith which could stand any test, and which was founded upon the rock.

While my friend went to seek a priest, who lived close by, I asked my clerical friend, by way of continuation of the former conversation, conscientiously where he thought the soul of our Saviour went, while His body was in the grave? to which he replied, "Certainly it went to limbo;" And where is limbo, said I; "Oh," says he, "no one knows that, we do not even know where heaven or hell is; but," said he, "I have *very peculiar* views myself upon the subject, for I believe in a *third state*, but, of course, I shall argue with the priest, *as if I did not so believe*, as it is common with Protestants."

The priest arrived, and the conversation took place, but how did my soul sink to witness the incapacity of my defender, as I had hoped he would be. Unable to defend his own faith, he could but attack the priest with isolated texts of Scripture, not bearing, to my mind, the least upon the subject. He lost his temper twice, and ended by a sentiment as unchristian as it was ungentlemanlike. The priest, on the other hand, was almost provokingly self-possessed and calm; he seemed conscious of possessing truth, and fearless for what he should advance. All he said was to the purpose. I could not shut my eyes to the contrast, though I would have given worlds to have been spared the bitter trial I saw before me; for all that presented itself to me was distress and bereavement, in the event of my becoming a Catholic, yet the true faith I was determined to embrace, and in the strength of God meet all that was before me. Without uttering a thought to human being, I went to my room and knelt down before God, and bound myself, from that hour, to learn what the Catholic faith really was, after which I took my pen and wrote the following, which my heart was bursting to give vent to, signing my name, as in the presence of God.

" This day, there was held a conversation

on controversial subjects, between my friend, the Rev. Mr. H—, and the Catholic priest, the Rev. Mr. R—g, in my presence. Up to this day, I was a staunch Protestant; I thought not, but that I was a child of Christ, after the true Scriptural sense, and that from Scripture, I, or at least my minister, could easily prove, that I belonged to Christ's Church, held the doctrines He left, and in short, followed Scripture with such precision as would shame Catholics, who professed to serve Christ, and still, (as I had always been led to believe) disregarded these same Scriptures.

" The conference began; my spiritual pastor, instead of showing an established mind regarding the sense of Scripture, was completely vanquished by the priest in point of argument, acknowledged he had peculiar views of Scripture, that perhaps, no other man had; whereas the priest instead of disregarding or not knowing Scripture, was so thoroughly acquainted with every line, and so established on every point, that he seemed to advance it with the simplicity, facility, and clearness of one who spoke the truth in his mother tongue. My friend denied, once or twice, he had said what I with my own ears had heard him say; he would not assent to points, nor could he from Scripture prove a *nay* to them. Therefore,

as a Protestant before God, I dare not but
protest, the priest was clear, stuck to Scripture
in his arguments, and had, to a *perfect degree*,
the power of defeating his opponent *from
Scripture*; that he was *calm*, *unruffled*, and
christian-like; said he came to speak the
truth, and that if he possessed it not, if the
Protestant would convince him that he had
truth, he would instantly become a Protestant;
whereas my friend was agitated, confused,
and bewildered, and ended by saying: ' *Those
are my opinions; and I care not what other
man living thinks!*' Alas! where was the
care for the soul, we should look for in Christ's
minister, and which I had hoped to find in
mine? I blush to say, I saw it in the
despised Catholic priest. I saw the com-
posure of the conscious possessor of truth with
him—a willingness to yield to conviction, if
it could be produced, where it could not, a
desire to convince. I therefore hereby declare, if I were to be guided by what I have
this day heard, I should at once become a
Catholic; but I will not yield up my native
faith, because *one* of my Protestant ministers
proclaims himself incapable of defending my
cause; no, but from this moment, I feel it
binding upon me to search the matter before
God; and I pray, if in being a Protestant I
am what God has revealed in Scripture we

ought to be, if we wish to dwell with Him
for ever, that He will strengthen me against
all argument, and against all endeavour to
lead me from what is pure and true; but if
the reviled and despised Romanists be of the
true Church of Christ, then I pray, oh, my
God, that all my prejudices may be overcome,
that I may by the power and truth of God
be persuaded, that my darkness (which I
thought was light) may be made manifest,
and that my mind and my heart may be
established in the way of truth, even to the
loss of all most dear upon earth—my own
flesh and blood. O my husband and my
children ! ! !—but Christ be my all.

FANNY MARIA PITTAR.

Feb. 10, 1842."

My mind being thus far relieved, I returned
to where my friend was sitting, determining
I would not allow him to know or see by my
manner, the effect produced within me. He
was to leave Edinburgh that night, and I
thought, if after I had made further search,
I should find it necessary to become a Catholic,
it would be quite time enough to tell him what
he had done for me. When about to leave
me, his parting words were, "Now, I hope
from what you have heard this morning, you

see the *fallacy* of these Catholic doctrines,
and how *unsatisfactory the meeting was*, therefore I beg that *on no account* you will ever
go again into a Catholic chapel, or talk upon
the subject again, as it cannot do you any
good." As I said before, for many reasons,
I did not wish him to know he had been the
means of making me fear and tremble, lest
my own doctrines were fallacious, not the
Catholic ones: therefore I simply replied:
Why not enter a chapel? Surely, the truth
we hold, if founded upon a rock, will only be
strengthened by hearing and thus proving the
errors of their creed. "Oh, said he, "you
must not seek for truth where there is nothing
but error." That, said I, I shall know and
be able to judge of, when I know what it is
they preach. We parted.

I now felt most anxious to find out, not
what was not Catholic doctrine, (for that
seemed to be all the progress I had hitherto
made,) but what it really was on the authority
of a priest; for although I was most desirous
to be able conscientiously to say, I thought
them in error, still I had the candour to
acknowledge (and act accordingly) that a
priest, not a Protestant minister, was the
person to apply to for this information; as a
greater mistake, or a greater injustice, was
never practised than to condemn a creed or

anything else on the testimony of its adversaries. To discover the real belief of Catholics, I therefore devoted much of my time; and as I each day and hour, gave myself to my bible, I found I progressed more and more towards Catholicity. In fact, from my own examination of Scripture, together with some little assistance from other sources, I found either that I must act up to my conscience, and become a Catholic, or yield to the troubles and trials I saw before me, and deny my Lord, to the eternal loss and misery of my precious immortal soul.

At this stage of my advance in Catholicity, I felt it due to my parents to acquaint them with what was passing in my mind, indeed I might say, was established in it; for, as I shall afterwards show by references to my bible, I felt that either I must become a Catholic, or part for ever from that book which was always dear to me, but now ten times more so than ever. It may not be amiss to copy a letter I wrote to my beloved parents at this trying moment, when I saw the awful necessity of, for the first time, acting in open violation of their wishes and the fearful possibility of incurring the displeasure, and perhaps more, of a most devoted husband. This communication may prove at least I did not lightly yield up my former opinions, but had a most bitter struggle before doing so; for indeed it was like tearing out my heart's core to wound such parents as mine, especially in the matter of religion, where I knew they considered me so firm. But I had the comfort of knowing if I should cause them pain, it was in the only matter I could do so, and still be blameless in the sight of God, the only authority I acknowledged superior to theirs, and therefore I could not, if I would but obey its call, come into the fulness of truth.

Edinburgh, Feb. 20—42.

" My Beloved Parents,

" The search I told you in my last letter, I was about to make, and which I dare not neglect or postpone, has been made, and what is the result? I find from proof beyond a doubt, and that from my precious Protestant Bible, that the Catholic religion not only looks likest Christ's religion and Church, *but actually is that Church.*

" What then am I to do? You have ever, I trust, found me a dutiful child, to the best of my ability willing, nay, anxious to show you both that obedience you deserve; in this step, therefore, I hope you will still find me yielding, as far as I possibly can, to your wishes.

I must now appeal to your reason. Have you not, on numberless occasions, applied to me for advice, nay, even direction in temporal matters, nevertheless, matters of importance to you, proving thereby that you considered me capable of some judgment and reason, and have I not, for the best part of my life, manifested an earnestness and sincerity for one thing more than all others, 'religion,' which insured for me more or less respect from you? Well, then, I ask you candidly, what has come over me now? Believe me, I am the very same in mind and body, as when I was with you, save that God has opened my eyes to a wondrous truth. Indeed, I am not mad, nor more a fool than when with you; but if you would not turn from one, that is the same as risen from the dead, you would at least hear me before you condemn me.

"For many years, (as many as twelve, for I remember what first drew my attention to it,) I have been earnestly desiring to find the God of the Bible, that He would become my Father, and all the blessings He has promised His children would become mine. Well, I did seek Him, and sometimes very earnestly, and with many tears, but I did not find Him. Sometimes I thought I had just attained a certainty, when, lo! it was gone. I neither felt it was with me, nor had I what is pro-

mised, and without which I could not be
happy. I kept my secret, and went to India,
every one supposing I was supported by a
power I felt I had not, and was further from
it than ever. There, where all around me was
dead and cold, I still felt the burning thirst
for a *sure and certain Saviour.* I never ceased
to seek, still I did not find. I knew I had as
much of Christ as my neighbours had, but I
felt I had not as much of Him as would
satisfy me, and as I felt He was willing to
give us, when He said He would *manifest*
Himself to those who sought Him; therefore,
I did, as Protestant ministers told me, and
also, as Presbyterians directed, and so on, but
no peace for me. The voice at last sounded
in my ears: How do you know you have
sought Him in the right religion? I saw some
hundred religions around me, all differing
widely, *and yet all drawn from the Bible!*
Now, what was I to do? I took my Bible in
my hand, and knelt down before God, and on
the truth of that word I supplicated He would,
sooner or later, *manifest* Himself to me, as
He had promised He would to those, who
persevered in seeking. I bound myself to
pray the words of Scripture, till God should
answer me, and show me where the truth
really was. I returned to England, and soon
after came to Edinburgh, with Protestant
4

books and Protestant arguments to lead my
friend, to whom I was going, from darkness,
(she being a Catholic;) but lo! in defending
my own faith, which I did as well as, and
better than hundreds could do, I saw, that
instead of darkness, she had found that light,
which will shine more and more unto the
perfect day. I resisted for a time, but I can
do so no longer. I see what I have been so
long in search of. I feel, at last, all my
prayers are answered. The truth is so perfect,
that it manifests itself, and I am so full of joy,
I can but pray and praise. All, that was dark
to me before in Scripture, is now as clear as
noon-day. I have found the pearl of great
price, I see its beauty, I experience its value,
and I reckon it will pay me for all I have to
suffer. Indeed, you might as well expect a
man starving with hunger, seated before a
banquet richly spread, to refrain from eating,
lest *possibly* the food might not satisfy him.
I see the marks Christ said should follow His
people, and Church, in Catholicity, and in
Catholicity alone, although it is *despised, a
very scorn to all men;* for as He was called
Beelzebub, how much more they. These
marks are with none but Catholics. Protestants are respected everywhere they go,
particularly their clergy, and *they are unanimous in but one thing, abuse of Catholics and*

their priests. This, then, cannot be a mark from Christ to them.

"Now, my dear parents, this treasure I have found, fills my soul with such rapture, such gratitude, and such peace, that I can but think of you all, and wish and pray, and pray and wish you may, each of you, yet possess it. I will now tell you what I have determined to do, previous to becoming a Catholic, for the satisfaction of your minds, and to prove to you *upon what* I have changed, and also my submission to you. I will go to the Protestant bishop of this place, and have Protestants present to judge, and if he can satisfy my mind, and shake my new faith, then I will never take that so much dreaded name; but to me it is even now inexpressibly dear, inasmuch as it bears my Saviour's mark, turn and examine it as I will.

"I have three things to ask you in justice to grant me; first, do not condemn me until you have heard me; secondly, from this time until I see you, cease not to pray that God will strengthen and defend you against all I may say, *if it be not truth, but if it be truth,* that He will open your eyes, touch your hearts, and overcome your scruples, so as to enable you to take that, which, though it may bring down scorn and reproach on your names, will, nevertheless, hereafter lead you to eternal life; then, thirdly, do not by word or deed seek to separate what God hath joined together; leave it to me to tell my husband of this change. Let no one speak to him of it. The God I have trusted so long, and at last found, will take me through deep waters; I am not afraid—I have summed up my account, and the balance is on my side. With many prayers, my best of parents, I commit you, with your other children to God.

"I must just mention to you the occasion of which I first yielded to God's grace, and determined to seek for myself, and discover what the Catholic faith really was. It was on hearing a discussion between a Protestant clergyman and a Catholic priest, who ought both to have known their own faiths, and that upon which they rested; but alas! for me, but *one* could give a reason from Scripture. The point discussed was their separate rules of faith. The one, I saw, neither knew his Bible, nor could he defend his faith from Scripture. He lost his temper twice, and when by the simplicity of truth, and the words of Scripture, he was unconsciously brought to a Catholic principle, he got off by saying, 'These are my opinions, sir, and I care not what any one else thinks!' This from a disciple of Christ, one who is to teach Christ's flock, and to strive in prayer for their precious souls! oh, I dare not longer resist, my hour was come. On the other hand, the priest was composed, unruffled, in the conscious possession of truth, and to this unchristianlike remark he mildly said, 'Then, sir, if you do not care for my soul, I care for yours, and if I cannot persuade you, do you try and persuade me, and I shall at once become a Protestant.' In short, all he said was to the purpose, and with that, he was humble and christianlike, so that I, who felt my precious soul depending on their words, finding my native faith as unstable as him who offered to defend it, submitted to God. I would also mention, that my clerical friend, and hitherto defender of my soul, having left Edinburgh, in a letter urges me to fly from this religion, not because he can prove it false, but because—why, I really blush to write it—because of *my husband, my children, and my friends.* How strange, when these are the very causes which urge me on! If I might hesitate about myself, when I think of these souls so inexpressibly dear to me, I could not, if I would, disregard the call. Besides, the Saviour I have found expressly tells me, I must leave *all, even these,* for His sake, if called to do it, and by the grace of God, I will do it, notwithstanding this appeal on my weakest point. With many tears and prayers for you all, believe me your affectionate child,

"FANNY MARIA PITTAR."

I shall now give a copy of my partial search of my Bible—partial it can but be, when I could only devote three or four days to it, and I find that every time I open my Bible, I have to add text upon text. My first object of search was for the Church, and what the marks were, by which it was to be discovered. The Catholic Church declaring itself to be that Church, and to be known to be such by its being *one, Holy, Catholic, Apostolic, and Infallible*, I determined to see how far these marks were supported by Scripture, and as far as I found them so, to respect them.

THE CHURCH.

Christ left a Church, and it was to be—

One.—Isaiah xxxv. 8, liv. 17, lx. 11, 12; Ezekiel xxxvii. 24, 26; Matt. xvi. 18, xviii. 17; John x. 16; Acts ii. 47, v. 11, viii. 1, xi. 26, xvii. 5, xiv. 27, xv. 22, xxviii. 22; Romans xvi. 4, 5; 1st Corinthians iv.

17; Coll. i. 18, 24; Ephesians i. 22, iv. 5, 13, 14, v. 25.

Holy.—Isaiah xxxv. 8, liv. 17; Malachi i. 11; Eph. v. 26, 27; Col. i. 18, 24.

Catholic.—Isaiah ii. 2, ix. 7; Daniel ii. 44; Malachi i. 11; Matt. xviii. 17, xxviii. 19, 20; Acts vii. 38; 1 Cor. i. 2; Ephesians iii. 2, 11, v. 32; Col. i. 17, 24; 1 Peter v. 13.

Apostolic.—Matt. xviii. 17, xxviii. 12, 20; Luke x. 2, 3, 16, xxii. 31, 32; John xv. 16, xvii. 18, 19, 20, 21, 22, 23; xx. 21, 23; Acts xv. 4; 1 Cor. xii. 2, 28; Eph. iv. 11, 12, 13, 14; Heb. xiii. 17; 1 John iv. 6.

Infallible.—Isaiah ii. 2, xxxv. 8, xl. 8, liv. 15, 17, lxix. 21, lx. 12; Ezekiel xxxvii. 26; Daniel ii. 44; Mich. iv. 7; Matt. xvi. 18, xxviii. 20; Mark xvi. 17; John xvi. 16, 17, 18, 26; Acts xix. 12; 1 Cor. xii. 28; Col. i. 16, 18, 24; Eph. i. 20, 21, iii. 9, 10, v. 24, 29; 1 Tim. iii. 15.

Having proved the points above stated so far scriptural, my desire naturally extended next to all the doctrines of that Church, which must surely be good and wholesome, if they emanated from the Church, upon which

the finger of God is so incontestably stamped.
I shall take them in the order they struck
myself, which is, first, the

Trinity.—Gen. xviii. 2, 3, 4; Matt. xxviii.
19; 2 Cor. xiii. 14; 1 John v. 7.

Pope, or Chief Bishop.—Matt. x. 2, 3, xvi.
18 ; Luke xxii. 31, 32; John xxi. 15, 16,
17 ; Acts i. 13, 15; xv. 7, 8, 9, 10, 11, 12.

Holy Orders.—Luke xxii. 19; John xx. 21,
22, 23; Acts vi. 5, 6, 7; xiii. 2, 3, 4;
1 Tim. iv. 14.

Tradition (Apostolic).—Deut. xxxii. 7; Matt.
xxviii. 20; Luke x. 16; John x. 16; xvii.
18; Acts xv. 17; xx. 28; 1 Cor. xi. 2;
2 Thes. ii. 15, iii. 6; 2 Tim. i. 13, 14,
ii. 2.

Scriptures (Not our sole rule of faith).—Matt.
xviii. 17; Acts xx. 28; xxvi. 33; 1 Cor.
i. 10; vi. 17; 2 Thes. ii. 16, iii. 6; 2
Peter iii. 6; i. 20; 2 Tim. i. 13, 14.

Baptism.—Matt. iii. 6; xxviii. 19; Mark xvi.
16; John iii. 5; Acts vii. 36, 37, 38 (and
faith one); Mark xvi. 16; Acts xiii. 48;
Gal. v. 6; Eph. iv. 5; Heb. xi. 6; James
ii. 14, 17.

Confirmation.—Acts xix. 6; John xx. 22; 2 Cor. i. 22; Heb. vi. 2.

Abstinence.—Gen. ii. 17; Exodus xii. 15; Lev. xi. 7, 8; Daniel x. 2, 3, 12; Acts xv. 28, 29.

Fasting.—Joel ii. 12, 13, 15; Daniel x. 2, 3, 12; Jonas iii. 5, 6, 7, 10; Matt. iv. 2, ix, 15; Mark ii. 20, ix. 27, 28, 29; Luke v. 35; Acts xiii. 2, 3, xiv. 23; 2 Cor. vi. 5, xi. 27.

Confession.—Numbers v. 5, 6, 7; Matt. iii. 5, 6, xviii. 18; John xx. 22, 23; Acts xix. 18; James v. 16; 1 John i. 8, 9.

Absolution.—Matt. ix. 6, xvi. 18, 19; John xx. 21, 22, 23; 2 Cor. ii. 10.

Councils (of the Church assisted by God).— Matt. xviii. 20; Acts xv. 28, 41.

Eucharist.—Matt. xxvi. 26, 27, 28; Mark xiv. 22, 24; Luke xxii. 19; John vi. 27, 32, 49, 50, 51, 52, 53, 54, 55, 56, 57, 60; 1 Cor. x. 16, xi. 26, 27, 28, 29; 2 Peter i. 4; Eph. v. 30; Col. i. 26, 27.

Free Will.—Gen. iii. 9; Deut. xxx. 19; Prov.

i. 24, 25; Isaiah v. 4; Ezekiel xviii. 31,
32; Matt. xxiii. 37; Luke xiii. 34; Acts.
vii. 51; Heb. xii. 15; 2 Peter iii. 9; Rev.
iii. 20.

Purgatory.—Isaiah xlix. 9, lxi. 1; Matt. v.
25, 26, xii. 32, 36; 1 Cor. iii. 13, 14, 15;
Eph. iv. 8.

To pray for the dead is said to be a good
and wholesome thought in 2 Maccabees xii.
43, 46. This portion of Scripture, though
not in all Protestant Bibles, is nevertheless in
some, and in all Catholic ones, so that we
cannot but respect it; besides we all know it
was, and is a custom with the Jews to pray
for their dead, and as our Lord taught so
often in their synagogues what they were to
do, and from what to refrain, we cannot but
suppose He would surely have prohibited this
practice, had it been either sinful or useless.

Hell (its torments eternal).—Isaiah xxxiii.
14; Mark ix. 42, 43, 44; Rev. xx. 9, 10.

Extreme Unction.—James v. 14, 15; Mark
vi. 13.

Sin (Original).—Psalms li. 5; Rom. v. 12;
Eph. ii. 3.

Mass, Prefigured by Melchisedech.—Gen. xiv.
18, 19, 20; Heb. v. 1, 2, 3, 6, 10, vii. 3,
15, 17, ix. 15, xiii. 10; Malachi i. 10, 11;
Luke xxii. 19, 20; 1 Cor. x. 16.

Indulgences, the power granted by Jesus to
St. Peter and his successors.—Matt. xvi.
17, 18, 19; John xx. 21, 22, 23; 2 Cor.
ii. 8, 10.

Images are sanctioned, nay, commanded of
God.—Exodus xxv. 18, 19; Num. xxi. 8,
9; 1 Kings vi. 23, 32. Relative honour
to be paid them, authorized, 2 Samuel xi.
12, 14, 15; Philip. ii. 9, 10.

Angels have charge over us.—Gen. xlviii. 16;
their aid to be sought, Exodus xxiii. 21, 22,
23; Zach. i. 12; Josue v. 14, 15, 16;
Matt. xviii. 10; Luke xv. 10; Heb. i. 14;
Rev. i. 4, viii. 3.

Saints, departed, equal to Angels.—Matt. xxii.
30; Mark xii. 25; Luke xvi. 9, xx. 36,
xv. 10; 1 Cor. xiii. 12; Acts xii. 7; 1
John iii. 2; Rev. ii. 26, v. 8; for invoca-
tion, 1 Kings vii. 8, 9, 10; Rom. xv. 30;
Heb. xiii. 18; James v. 16, *Relics.*

Relics.—2 Kings xii. 20; 21; Matt. ix. 20,

21, 22; Acts v. 15, 16, xix. 11, 12.
Blessed Virgin the Mother of God.—Isaiah
ix. 6; Matt. i. 23; Luke i. 35, 40, 41, 42,
43, 44, 45, 46, 47, 48, 49.

Continency, both possible and profitable.—Deut.
xxiii. 21; Matt. xiv. 11, 12; 1 Cor. vii.
7, 8, 2, 32, 33; 1 Tim. v. 11, 12.

Convents, sanctioned and recommended by
Scripture.—Matt. xix. 21, 27, 29; Luke
xiv. 33; 1 Cor. vii. 34, 35, 37, 38, 40.

Works, good works meritorious.—Gen. iv. 6,
7, xxii. 16, 17, 18; Psalm xviii. 20, xix.
11; Matt. v. 11, 12, x. 42, xiv. xxvii;
Rom. ii. 6, iv. 5; 1 Cor. iii. 8; 2 Tim.
iv. 8.

Just at this time, letters came pouring in
upon me from those of my friends who knew,
either from myself or others, the state of my
mind, to beg and entreat of me to read my
Bible, and to humble myself, as pride was the
cause of my fall. All this I did as they recommended. As far as regards Scripture, the
proof lies before me, to which I did not fail to
add the most earnest prayer my soul could
offer up, that I might be strengthened against
Catholicity, *if it were false.* As I said before,

I have given proof that I did not neglect my
Bible in my distress, but what did I find
there?—Catholicity in every line.   Where
was I, or where were my senses, when as a
Protestant I had read over and over again all
those passages without seeing anything in
them to raise a doubt in my mind?   I shook
myself, as one awakening out of a deep sleep,
so deep, it had well nigh ended in death.
This very something, that has passed over
myself in the short space of four or five
days, prepared me for greater things, although
I could not tell what it was, or how it had been
effected; still, that there was a change, I was
certain.   I could no more account, how it had
been wrought, than the man who was ques-
tioned how he came to see, having been born
blind.   His reply was, what mine must be,
" I cannot tell, I only know, that whereas I was
born blind, I now see."   I cannot tell, indeed,
how it is that I now see in my Bible, which I
have read hundreds of times, and studied hard,
what I never saw before.   The substance truly
is changed, though the appearance remains the
same.   I cannot think my Bible has been in-
terlined with Catholic doctrines, by wily
priests, as they are called; that I know to be
impossible, for the book has never been out of
my possession; but even if it had, its unaltered
appearance must prove that man had nothing

to do with it. The ability thus to change the
substance, while the appearance remains the
same, I am forced to trace to a Divine power,
which has thus graciously prepared a way in
my heart for the reception of another and more
blessed belief, even that of the most Holy Eucharist. Yes, I do believe, the substance I
receive is the very Body and Blood of my
crucified Lord. I believe it, simply because
He says it, and because I feel in myself the
effects of such heavenly food. When my
Saviour says, *"This is My Body,"* and,
" This is My Blood," and " except ye eat of
My Body and *drink My Blood,* ye can have
no life in you ;" and again, " He that eateth
Me, even He shall live by *Me ;"—I believe,*
I cannot help it. Christ came to save us, and
give us life, and if we cannot have life, unless
we eat Him, then He died in vain, unless we
can get Him to eat, or else He spoke not
truth, which is blasphemy to suppose, when
He said, we could not have life unless we eat
Him. John vi. 53. What then am I, a
Bible reader, to do when such passages as
these stare me in the face? Also, 1 Cor. xi.
29, St. Paul speaking of communicating unworthily, says, " We eat damnation to ourselves, not discerning the Body of the Lord."
What then am I to do? Certainly to seek
where I can get that blessed Body—and where

is that? Nowhere but in the Catholic Church.
Besides, must I not argue from the above,
that if there be *no Body*, as Protestants say,
then St. Paul must have been wrong; or if
he is right, then the others must be wrong,
and I suppose, as I am a Protestant, and born
to the happy privilege of judging for myself, I
may bring in which I choose, as the erring
party. Again, can it be possible that God,
who is so merciful and just, would damn us
for not discerning what is not there to be discerned? Oh no, no. The Jews said to our
Lord: "But *how* can it be?" and so says the
Protestant; but does not our Lord answer
their *how*, and clear up their doubts and difficulties, as He was ever wont to do, where the
case would admit of it, as in the case where
He declared that to enter the kingdom of
heaven we must be born again? Nicodemus
said: "But, Lord, how can this be?" John, iii.
4. Jesus *instantly explained*, that He did not
mean literally, that a man was to enter his
mother's womb, and be born a second time,
but that he was to be born of water and the
spirit. But in this case, our Lord answers
their *how* by increasing the difficulty. He
simply says: "*Except ye eat Me, ye shall have
no life in you;*" and when they said, "*This
is a hard saying,*" He said, "Doth this offend
you? How much more difficult will it be to

believe what I have said, when ye see My body ascend with Me to where I was before, and still, if you do not believe it, ye have no life in you." Yes, I do believe it, (blessed be God); I believe that He, who made all things out of nothing, can make Himself present when and where He pleases. To a Protestant, and a Jew, who have not faith, it is indeed a *hard saying;* to me, though I feel most unworthy of having been brought to the true and real faith of Christ, it is life and peace. A Protestant clergyman said to me: "And is it possible you have fallen so far in so short a time, as to believe a doctrine not only blasphemous, but so thoroughly contrary to human reason?" It is not impossible, said I, to a power to whom nothing is impossible. I believe it, and my greatest glory is, that I am able to say I do so. I may add, I believe it in the same way I believe the incarnation of our Lord. *The one is as unintelligible to the human mind as the other.*

But not my Bible alone has become metamorphosed to me: *my Protestant Prayer-Book* has likewise gone through a change. At least, I see it now in quite a different light to what I once did; and when I reflect upon the matter, I cannot help thinking of those passages in Scripture, which I have so often read, and wondered what they could mean;

Matt. xiii. 14, 15; Mark, iv. 12; Luke, viii.
10; John, xii. 40. "Therefore, they could
not believe," because that Isaiah said again,
"He hath blinded their eyes, and hardened
their hearts, that they should not see with their
eyes, nor understand with their hearts, and be
converted, and I should heal them." My
Prayer-Book now seems to me the best book
I could choose to place in a Protestant's
hands, *for close examination*, to prove the
truth, the *purity*, and the *consistency of the
Catholic religion*, and why, I will now tell you.
A Protestant clergyman, trying to frighten me
out of my admiration of my beautiful and
spotless Church, assures me, assuming a serious
face, the subject being so awful, that one *shock-
ing practice* of the Catholic Church, introduced
into it by priests, for bad purposes, *is confession of sins*, after which, they gull the people
by giving them *absolution!* Now, not to speak
of the testimony I have given upon this subject from my Bible, I open my Prayer-Book,
and I see, that previous to receiving the sacrament, and at a sick bed, the minister is to
press the person to make *a full confession of sin*,
and afterwards *to give him absolution!* What
absurdity is this in a Protestant's mouth!
They who dissent from the Episcopal Church,
and condemn the practice of confession, are
consistent people so far, but, for Episcopalians,

5

and *their ministers* to abuse a doctrine and
practice as unscriptural, and imposed upon
Catholics by their priests, when every Protestant minister is obliged to declare he will
practise it, before he can be ordained [*see the
Ordination Service,*] and every lay person,
who frequents a church, or uses a Prayer-
Book, thereby assents to the principle, is an
absurdity so monstrous that before I can
respect such teachers, who profess one thing
and *do diametrically the opposite,* it must be
proved to me, I do not understand my mother
tongue.

Then, again, I am told the Catholic
Church, among her other self-assumed powers,
commands *fasting.* Well, Scripture apart
again, on this point, even the express command of our Saviour Himself, Matt. ix. 15,
Mark ii. 20, I open my *Prayer Book,* and I
find " *A Table of the Vigils,* (a thing I never
heard of as a Protestant,) *Fasts,* and *Days of
Abstinence !* to be observed during the year,"
and as I think what follows so almost incredi-
ble, I would advise all to refer to their Prayer
Book, to see that I am making no mistake.
But as the book may not be at hand, I shall
give a copy of what I can myself hardly persuade myself I see aright.

DAYS OF FAST AND ABSTINENCE.

THE EVENS OR VIGILS BEFORE

The Nativity of our Lord.	St. John Baptist.
The Purification of the B.V.	St. Peter.
Mary.	St. James.
The Annunciation of the B.	St. Bartholomew.
V. Mary.	St. Matthew.
Easter Day.	St. Simon and St. Jude.
Ascension Day.	St. Andrew.
Pentecost.	St. Thomas.
St. Matthias.	All Saints.

1st. The forty days of Lent.
2nd. The Ember days at the four Seasons.
3rd. The three Rogation Days, being the Monday, Tues-
, day, and Wednesday, before Holy Thursday, or the
Ascension of our Lord.
4th. All the Fridays in the year except Christmas day.

NOTE.—That if any of these feast days fall upon a
Monday, then the Vigil or Fast Day shall be kept upon
the Saturday, and not upon the Sunday next before it.—
Pure Catholicity.

Now, will any one really believe that the
above is copied from the Protestant Prayer
Book?—and yet it is true, and can be proved
so by referring to the book. All I know is,
when I was first told it was there, I would
not credit it, and now that I see it, it is as
much as I can do to credit my eyes. I also
see it enjoined on the clergyman to declare
after Communion what fast days are to be

observed during the ensuing week; also, that all persons prepare themselves for the holy state of Matrimony by *abstinence* and *fasting*: and in the Collect for the first Sunday in Lent, I see a prayer addressed to God, to beg grace to use such *abstinence*, and to do that for which they not only condemn, but thoroughly despise Catholics. *What mocking of God! What inconsistency!* I ask any honest candid person, is this a .Church one can fearlessly adhere to, and on the *truth, stability*, and *consistency* of which they will stake their precious souls? Its ministers profess what they do not practice; for if they practice fasting they do not preach it, and if they dared preach it, who would believe they practised it? But this is not all:—Tell me, Protestant reader, if you are possessed of one iota of candour, what passes in your mind when you hear the word *penance?* a Catholic doing penance! Now, acknowledge it is a word you have nothing to do with, that it belongs only to poor deluded Catholics, and if your heart be a tender one, tell me how you could weep for motives so misguided, and so deceived. But before the tears have left your eyes, let me ask you to open your Prayer Book at that part called " A Commination," and you will read as follows, after which reserve your tears for yourself:—" Brethren, *in the primitive*

Church there was a Godly discipline, that at the beginning of Lent, such persons as stood convicted of notorious sin, were put to open *penance, and punished in this world, that their souls might be saved in the day of the Lord;* and that others, admonished by their example, might be the more afraid to offend. Instead whereof, *until the said discipline may be restored again, which is much to be wished!''* &c. Tell me now, reader, who needs your tears most?—Catholics, who are *obliged* to practice what their religion teaches, or lose the reward it holds out, or yourselves, who are reared in ignorance of the true faith, the only one consistent in all things?

But the *inconsistency* of Protestantism does not stop here. Every Sunday they are obliged to declare they believe in " *One Holy, Catholic, and Apostolic Church, the Communion of Saints, and the forgiveness of sins,''* &c. Now, I would ask, is that Church Catholic which is only three hundred years old, when there is one from which it emanated, eighteen hundred years old? Or is that Church *Apostolic* which dissented from *the Ancient Church,* and was obliged to ordain its ministers after a *new fashion?* Or what is this *Communion of Saints,* that very Communion for which Catholics are a scorn and a derision among Protestants? And this *for-*

giveness of sins,—what does it mean, that Protestants can say they believe in it? It is the leaven of Catholicity which God has left in the Protestant Church, whereby to draw sincere souls into His own most beautiful and consistent Church. And surely every Protestant ought to blush on reciting this creed, when *Luther*, the head and founder of the Reformation (falsely so called), out of which their Church has sprung, has left on record, and by Protestant writers recorded too, that when he first severed himself from the Catholic Church, he stood alone in the world, no other man living holding the same views or faith that he did.

But I have not done yet. I must point out a few more inconsistencies in the Protestant Prayer Book, before I can bring myself to leave the subject, as these lines may meet the eye of some poor Protestant, as sincere as I was myself, and who may, by the power of God, be led to truth through the very matters I am now treating of.

To commence again, then we will notice first the general confession of sin which almost immediately begins the service. *The priest* (mark he is no priest at all according to Scripture, for we are told in Heb. v. 1, 2, 3, a priest must offer sacrifice for sin, and the idea, we all know, is obnoxious to all Protes-

tants) pronounces *absolution* upon all the people, whether they be penitent or not. Now
mark, this if it means anything at all, it is
practising (if we may use such a term where
nothing is performed) the very power Catholics are abused for using, and which is
charged upon them as an invention of their
priests. Now, I would ask any Protestant if
he has ever gone to church particularly bur-
dened with some sin or other, or with sin in
general, has he felt, after these words are pronounced, as if perfectly forgiven by God, and
in consequence perfectly relieved? Or does
he feel, as I always did, that these were mere
empty words, without any healing power?
Or I would suppose the case of a murderer
being present, and that he has joined in the
general confession. If any one present be
absolved, so is he, and can any one suppose
such a crime pardoned at such a tribunal, and
absolved by *the priest*, who is perfectly ignorant of the mighty work he has just performed, that of having reconciled a soul to its
God, before at deadly enmity?

Another inconsistency is, that after the
" Te Deum" in the " Benedicite," they not
only address the angels, for which they cannot
find language strong enough to abuse the
Catholics, but they adjure the spirits and souls
of the faithful departed; as for instance,

"*Ananias, Azarias, and Misael,* bless ye the
Lord." They will say they have Scripture
authority for this—so they have; but let
them know their Bibles better, before they
condemn others for what they themselves do,
or ought to do, if their Prayer Book is to
direct them—*that borrowed book,* which they
only hold to bear testimony against them.

Another monstrosity in the mouth of a Protestant is " Saint Athanasius's Creed." Many
have staggered at the recital of this; would to
God they had staggered until they had fallen
upon truth and consistency. The Protestants
profess such charity towards the souls of all
men, that let their lives have been what they
may, if they can only be got to pronounce
the name of Jesus on their death-beds, they
are instantly pronounced safe in the highest
heavens; whereas, in this creed, they boldly
pronounce none safe but such as hold the
Catholic faith, which said faith they themselves neither hold actually nor nominally.
That they do not hold it actually, this little
pamphlet is written to prove; that they do
not hold it nominally, I will give you a little
proof of.

The first time I visited Kingstown, after
my conversion, my first desire was to know
where my magnet (the Catholic Church)
lay. I approached some poor creatures on

the road side, and said, Can you tell me
where the Catholic Church is? at which one
old woman stood up and said, " Look, jewel,
do you see the sign of redemption there, the
crass (cross) that always marks the *Catholic
Church;* and if you want the Protestant
Church, dear, look for a *weather cock*, and
you won't be far astray!"

They also declare in the same creed, that
"they that have *done good* shall go into *everlasting life;* and they that have *done evil* into
everlasting fire." Now, when poor Catholics
urge this upon their own people, these very
Protestants say, here is a pretty religion,
trusting to their works for salvation. Oh,
Protestants, Protestants! what a privilege to
be freed from the title.

Again, look at the Litany, and you will see
another token of Catholicity, just enough to
show that they who Protestantized, and borrowed the Prayer Book, (for in many things
it is an exact copy of the Missal,) had not
sufficiently forgotten their original faith; for
therein they pray, " from fornication and all
other deadly sins, good Lord deliver us;" that
is, good Lord deliver us from what we de-
nounce Catholics for saying there exist—
deadly sins!

Next come the Collects. In the third Sunday in Advent, they pray, " that the minis-

ters and stewards of *Thy mysteries*," &c.
What mysteries? Whatever wise head penned
this collect, forgot he was henceforth to *protest* against the *mysteries of the old religion.*
There is no mystery in bread and wine. But
when that bread and wine become, by the
power of God, " Christ," whole and entire,
human and divine,—here is something like a
mystery, a mystery that has triumphed over
all difficulties, and has outlived, and ever
must outlive all (falsely so called) Reforma-
tions.

Then again, in the sixth Sunday after Epi-
phany they pray " that they may purify
themselves, *even as He is pure*," and when Catholics strive at such an attainment, they
shrug their shoulders in pity and disgust, and
exclaim, Poor misguided self-righteous Phari-
sees!

Next comes Ash-Wednesday (dear Ash
Wednesday). After the collect, there is a
command given, that it is to be read *every day*
in Lent. Where?—not in the churches, for
they are not open. Then the epistle is read
as follows :—" Turn ye, saith the Lord, to
Me, with all your heart, and with *fasting*."
So the Lord has ordered them to do what
they pity and despise the Catholics for doing.
Oh, happy consistent Catholics, a few more
scoffs, and a few jeers, and you will meet the

reward of your steady and constant adherence
to the known commands of your God.

Look next at the Collect, "*St. Michael and
all angels.*"   " O everlasting God, &c. merci-
fully grant, that as the holy angels do Thee
service in heaven, so by Thy appointment
they may succour and defend us on earth,
through Jesus Christ our Lord."   I thought
it was only superstitious Catholics could suppose the holy angels could help them; but
here is a proof of the contrary, notwithstanding, it strikes me as a mighty queer subject
for a Protestant Collect.

Next comes All Saints day. " O Almighty
God, who hast *knit together Thine elect in one
communion, in the mystical body of Thy Son
Christ our Lord, grant us grace so to follow
Thy blessed saints in all virtues and goodly
living, &c.*"   Now mark, first, " one communion," and as there are some hundred
Protestant communions, this passage can never
be intended for themselves.   Secondly, they
pray for grace to follow the example of the
saints, and when Catholics urge the same,
they ridicule them for it.   They also despise
fasting and confession, which the saints could
not live without.

Again, I cannot but remark upon an order
just after the communion service, that unless
there be three or four to communicate with

the priest, there shall be *no communion*, so that *one* or *two* souls may thirst, and thirst again, to unite themselves in communion to their Saviour, but it will be all in vain, unless there be found more so disposed. Perhaps they calculate that two souls are not worth the bread and wine used upon the occasion, but for three or four that expense can be gone to. I cannot think of any other reason. There is also another order, which is, that every parishioner shall communicate at least three times a year, Easter to be one. What a leaven of Catholicity, copied out of the Catholic catechism. I most solemnly declare, in all my Protestant career, I never heard the above urged upon us, as a duty, or even recommended particularly as a practice.

Lastly, let me direct your attention to the pretty little apology, with which the communion service ends. For kneeling, while communicating, it says, " lest through *ignorance* or *infirmity*, or out of *malice* or *obstinacy*, persons should misconstrue the matter, it is hereby declared that no adoration is intended to the bread and wine, as that were idolatry, to be abhorred of all Christians," &c. Then comes a very wise assertion, that Christ's natural body *cannot be in two different places at the same time ;* and yet it could pass through a stone wall, which is equally at variance with the laws of nature. But perhaps the Bible makes a mistake when it says so, for the *Prayer Book* says it is contrary to reason to suppose such a thing possible. I must still further point out the Catholic rite, with which a Protestant child is baptized, "*signed with the sign of the cross*," for which absurdity they again apologize in the following words: "To take away all scruples concerning the use of the sign of the cross in baptism; the true explication thereof, and the just reasons for the retaining of it, may be seen in the 30th Canon, *first published in the year* 1604."

Now, for one peep at the Catechism. The question is asked, "what is the *inward sign* of the Sacrament of the Lord's Supper?" Answer: "*The body and blood of Christ,* which are *verily* and *indeed taken and received* by the faithful in the Lord's Supper." *The. Holy Ghost* has said of the Church, that he that runs may read, and the wayfaring man, *though a fool cannot err therein;* now, I would ask any Protestant, supposing him not to be a fool, how he would understand these words, "*verily and indeed taken and received.*" I know I would take them as the Catholic does, and as the words imply; but the Protestant says we err therein, *though the Holy Ghost says we cannot !!*

Now, hear how the Catechism closes. "The *curate of every parish* shall diligently upon *Sundays* and *holydays*, after the second lesson at evening prayer, openly in the church instruct and examine so many children as he shall think convenient, in some part of this Catechism." Is this done? no, it is not, that ever I saw, except in catholic Churches, the difference being, that the commands of the one Church are attended to, in the other they are only a dead letter, left in it to perfect the condemnation of her unhappy adherents.

I was thus led by the two highest authorities into Catholicity, namely, *my Bible and Prayer Book*, for mind, I have not been abusing the Prayer Book, for I think there is a *vast deal* of sound sense and doctrine in it, just so far as there is Catholic doctrine in it; no, but it is Protestants I find fault with, for *professing what they condemn others for doing.* But I still shrank from becoming a Catholic, *if it were possible to avoid it*, and my enemy did not fail to suggest it was not necessary; besides which, by nature I was disinclined towards it, for, on the one hand, there was my easy-going Protestant faith, which practically said, to me, eat drink, and be merry; while, on the other side, everything was against my nature : confession to be made constantly of *every secret sin*, whether in *thought*, *word*, or *deed:* regular humiliation of the flesh, in fasting and abstinence: the cross to be borne, which even then, I could see was sizeable: the despised name of Catholic to be taken, together with a world of woe : perhaps to be deserted by all dear to me on earth. Indeed, I would have given worlds to have been able to discard this new found religion. I therefore determined, as a last resource, to try and find out exactly what the Protestant rule of faith was; for although I had been reared in it, and managed to pass in the world as a sincere good Protestant, still I could not trust to myself ; for I found that all the points which I had considered quite settled, and firm as a rock, when tried by this Catholic touchstone, *shook, tottered, and fell !*

I inquired, therefore, of a Protestant clergyman, what the Protestant rule of faith was! I was answered, "the Bible." Is it infallible? "Certainly," was the reply. Well, said I, is it your only rule of faith ? "Yes," again was the reply. Then, said I again, you profess to do all it commands, and to abstain from all it forbids; neither to add to, nor diminish? "Yes," was the answer. And at that my heart sank, for I saw, on opening my Bible, *a strict command*, under the *Patriarchal law*, the *Jewish law*, and lastly, the *Christian law*, to keep the Sabbath, or *seventh* day holy, Christ Himself gave example so to do; for we are told in Luke iv. 16: " As His custom was, He went into the Synagogue on the *Sabbath* day, and read to the people." Luke xxiii. 56. How then, was naturally my next question, is it that Protestants keep the *first* day, and not the *seventh*, as God has so expressly ordered in the Bible? and on examination I found many, many commands to keep it, but *not one to change the day.* My clerical friend then said, " Protestants keep the first day instead of the seventh, because they see from Scripture, the Apostles met on the first day, to pray and break bread." I look to my Bible again, and find they did; but I also find, they met on the *second* day, as well. Acts xx. 11.—Now why not keep Monday holy, as the authority for the one day is as good as for the other; therefore, how can this be authority to change so positive a command of God? If one person would think it satisfactory or sufficient, one hundred others would not think so; therefore, this cannot be the reason, at least not an *infallible* one, and nothing else could cancel a command so continuously and so solemnly given by God, and adhered to by our Lord Himself. Just as my mind was perplexed on this point, I came across a work just published by an eminent Presbyterian divine, the Rev.

John Bruce, entitled "The Duty and Privilege of Keeping the Sabbath." After endeavouring to prove the grounds of the change of days, from the seventh to the first, he finds it necessary to sum up thus: "In other words, you would reasonably suppose or expect the change should be gone into, which the *Christian Church* affirms hath actually taken place." —p. 32. Here is Protestant authority to guide me! If I felt timid to trust to myself, and to yield to my own doubts, here is a Protestant divine who tells me, the *best authority for the change* is the *Church's* having ordered or sanctioned it, in other words, *tradition;* that, for which the good gentleman thought fit to separate and dissent from the Christian Church for holding; and here, he tells us, this is the all-sufficient reason for this great change. I believe he never spoke truer words, but, from him, surely, they are the height of inconsistency. Some may here say, —but Catholics keep the first day as well as we. Yes, they do, but they know why they do so; they keep it from the authority recommended by the worthy gentleman above, which authority he does not acknowledge, and scorns to be influenced by. On mentioning the above to my friend Mr. H., he begged I would not suffer any uneasiness, on account of the change from the Sabbath to the first day,

6

for, said he, " I can prove to you by a *most
beautiful and clear calculation,* that the day
we keep holy is *actually the very same day the
Patriarchs kept for their Sabbath.*"   This was
quite a new idea, and presented to my mind a
hope, which realized about as much peace to
my soul, as a straw held out to a drowning
man would do; he would grasp at it, but
would it save him?   No; no more could the
proof that I had *actually* been doing right, by
observing the day without knowing it, be a
sufficient reason to prevent me becoming a
Catholic.

Another strict command I saw given at all
times, even up to the Christian council at
Jerusalem, " that all *Christians abstain, as a
necessary thing, from eating blood,*" Acts xv.
22, whereas I see all Protestants partake of it
without scruple.   Who refrains, I would ask,
on this account, from eating wild fowl? and
yet we all know the blood remains in them;
or who from black-pudding and such dishes?
No one, that ever I saw.   Thus, Protestants,
I find, are not consistent either in their profession, or their practice: they do not live
by, or up to their rule of faith, the Bible.
Catholics have no scruples in eating blood, but
they know why they can do so, without a
breach of this command.   They have the
Bible 'tis true, and they have besides, an

authority emanating from the same source,
and therefore, the only authority capable of
nullifying a command therein given from that
authority, "the Church," or the "word
spoken," as St. Paul tells us, 2 Thess. ii. 14.
They are authorised to eat blood, and by the
same authority Protestants partake of it,
though they do not know it, or if they did,
they dare not say so, for it would be acknow-
ledging Catholic authority. I mentioned
these subjects to many, who were concerned
for the progress I was making towards Catholicity, just to see if any of them could help
me out of my doubts, and they one and all
startled and asked me, was I allowing *such
trifles* to unsettle my mind? But I would ask
such, can anything *God has commanded as
necessary be a trifle?* or are these commands
more trifling or differing in their nature, from
that laid upon our first parents, under pain of
death, to abstain from eating a certain
fruit, and yet, from the punishment incurred,
can any urge or argue the fault to have been a
trifling one? Oh, reader, look at the results,
and by them learn to appreciate *trifles*, when
God issues them!

Having received my clerical friend's *beautiful* and *clear* solution, which I consider myself
fortunate in having obtained upon paper, in
his own handwriting, or else who would credit

me, that a clergyman of the English Church
could put forth such an assertion, I cannot
resist the temptation of giving a copy of it
here, to let the reader judge of its *beauties*,
and to show to what purposes the Holy Scriptures can be wrested, when once they are left
to the judgment of man to construe, as he
pleases.

"THE PATRIARCHAL AND CHRISTIAN SABBATH
CELEBRATED ON ONE AND THE SAME DAY
OF THE WEEK.

"Exodus ii. 11, and xxxi. 17, order the
observance of the 7th day, in remembrance of
the Creation; Deut. v. 15, in remembrance of
the deliverance from Egypt, without any reference to the Creation.

" If the Israelites had left Egypt on the day
which had previously been observed as the
Sabbath, in remembrance of the Creation, we
might conclude that this passage contained an
additional reason for the observance of this
same day; but if they left Egypt on the day
before the usual Sabbath, then it can be viewed
in no other light than as an injunction to ob-
serve their Sabbath on a different day, and for
a different reason.

" That the Israelites left Egypt on the day

before the Sabbath is thus proved: 'They arrived at the Wilderness of Sin on the 15th day of the second month,' Exodus xvi. 1; 'The sixth day from that day was the day before the Sabbath,' v. 5 and 23, and the 20th day of the month; consequently, the 21st was the Sabbath, and the 22nd was the day after the Sabbath. If we reckon back we shall find that the 15th, the 8th, and the 1st days of this month were also the days after the Sabbath; and so that the 30th and last day of the preceding month Abib, which is called the first month, was the Sabbath day, and consequently the 29th, the 22nd, and the 15th days, were the days before the Sabbath, but the 15th was the day on which the Israelites left Egypt. Numbers, xxxiii. 3.

"I wish, my dear friend," he concludes, "that all that has been stated to you by Romish priests, *was equally capable of that clear demonstration which I have given you above!*"

As I said before, I leave those who read these lines, to judge of their clearness and beauty. To me it appears, if anything is proved, it is that Friday ought to be the day kept holy; but, suppose, for argument's sake, his point is proved, then it follows that the whole Christian world has mistaken the seventh day of the week for the first, while the whole Jewish world must have mistaken the 6th of the week for the 7th; for, unquestionably, our Christian Sabbath is kept on the day immediately following the Sabbath of the Jews; therefore, if our Sabbath be still the seventh day, and not the first day of the week, as the Christian world has always supported it, then the whole Christian world has been wrong from the beginning; and if our Christian Sabbath be still the seventh day, and not the first, as it is certainly the day immediately following the Sabbath of the Jews—then the Jewish Sabbath must have been on the sixth day of the week, or *Friday*, and not the seventh day (Saturday); thus it follows, the Jews were all wrong, as well as the Christians, and nobody is right but my friend Mr. H.; and yet, Mr. H. believes that Christ died on Friday, or the eve of the Jewish Sabbath, and keeps *Good Friday* accordingly; and moreover, Mr. H. believes that our Saviour kept the Jewish Sabbath, *as the Sabbath*, and the proper one, and therefore, Mr. H., to be consistent, must believe that Christ Himself was wrong upon the subject !

Well, indeed might he, and every other friend I have in the world, bemoan over me, if all I have learnt from priests, and adopted from my soul, to the exclusion of every other hope, could be no better proved, or clearly

demonstrated, than what is stated above.
Yes, common tears would be but a poor offering at such a shrine; *tears of blood would not
be too much for a soul so lost.*

Many other Protestant inconsistencies I
could enumerate—things which they do not
authorize in Scripture, and things which they
neglect, therein commanded, as the *oneness* and
unity amongst them, which is well exemplified
in the *varieties* of ways they dealt with me.
I may as well instance a few things more, in
order to prove my assertions.

Infant baptism—where is the command in
Scripture for it? nowhere; on the contrary,
the Bible says, to be baptized we must *believe,*
and that, we all know, no child can do; and
yet the Protestant pretends to adhere to the
Bible, and denounces without mercy the
Catholic whom he is pleased to consider as
taught to neglect the Bible. But I would ask
him, why he baptizes his child? He cannot
tell why he does it, only he does it, and
would not for the world leave it undone.
Nor does his minister know why he makes the
sign of the cross upon the head of the child
when baptizing it, nor can he tell why it is
necessary that it should be apologised for in
the Prayer-Book; but both the one and the
other, whether they know it or not, depend
upon the authority of the Catholic Church.

. Then, again, Protestants say, the Scriptures are infallible ; *so they are, but not to them.* To be infallible, they must be infallibly interpreted, and not according to the *fruitful* and *frenzied fancy* of every presumptuous mind that declares itself directed by God to unfold them.   In this declaration I am supported by Scripture, 2 Peter, iii. 16.   "There are certain things in Scripture hard to be understood, which the unlearned and unstable, *wrest (as they do also the other Scriptures) to their own destruction.*"   Nevertheless, the unlearned, yea, *all, all*, are pronounced by the Protestant faith to be fit and perfectly capable of interpreting for themselves, whereas, Scripture expressly tells them, they do so to their own destruction.   Is this infallibility ?   But even if these passages were not in holy writ, to attest against the abuse to which the Scriptures have been brought by the Protestant faith, would not the effect produced by every one judging for himself, prove it to be an invention of man ?   Can God be the author of confusion ?   Does He give a rule of faith, and pronounce it infallible, in order to lead men to unity and oneness, and then direct them to form some hundred faiths, beliefs, and religions upon it.   Never, never! reason, sense, and Scripture, all pronounce it impossible. But if such be the Protestant rule of faith,

then, I ask any person with one iota of justice
in his composition, how, after what I have
produced from my Bible, can I be blamed
for the change I have made?   Happy, happy
change!

But, to give a clearer proof of how completely the Protestant system overturns the
infallibility of Scripture, and turns it into a
floodgate of error and untruth, I will give a
slight sketch of my own experience.

Born a member of the Episcopal Church, I
was happy as such for many years of my life,
never dreaming but my Church was the true
one, founded upon a rock; the idea of its not
being such never once entered my head.
Time passed, and I was obliged to change my
residence, but in doing so, I found I must lose
the best part of my religion, not being able to
bring my minister with me, for it seemed to
me, the best part of religion centered in him,
not in the Church.   He was a good man, and
I could find no piety like his.   In distress
about my soul, I looked about me for something to come up to my ideas of religion, and
by chance fell upon a class of Protestants
called "Wesleyan Methodists."   Here I saw
greater devotion, more frequent attendance at
their churches, greater helps to devotion and
serving God, though differing widely from the
interpretation of Scripture I had heard in my

former Church. However, I determined to use what they had to offer, until I could find better, not, however, to become one of them; the inducements were not quite sufficient for that. Time rolls on, and I am again forced to move my dwelling. In this place, I could find no Methodist Church, nor anything belonging to them; here again I was all in a puzzle. However, I set upon a search again, and at last decided there was real religion, in appearance at least, amongst another branch of the fruitful tree of Protestants called "Presbyterians." I followed this persuasion for a little time, because *I fancied* they preached sounder gospel than was to be had in the Episcopal Church of the place where I was, but the thought never crossed my imagination of becoming one of them, for I saw nothing to enable me to say, here is the truth which I can give a reason for professing.

At last I change my home again, (for I have seen a great deal of the world), and am again in a puzzle to know where to direct my steps to the goal of truth. The thought naturally presented itself, *truth is one*, therefore these three persuasions that I have lately had to do with cannot be all right, because they widely differed from each other. The Bible told me, Christ had left *one faith*, one Church, and one baptism, and the question is, where is this Church? The Wesleyan minister tells me his is it; that he had prayed and prayed again, and that *God* had taught him to understand Scripture as taught by his Church. The Episcopalian minister says, "No, my Church is it, for I have prayed as well and longer than he has, and my Church was an old one before his was in existence." Then says the Presbyterian minister: "Never mind either of them, for if they have prayed long, I have prayed better, and *God* has taught me that *I only am right.*"

Now, these are all Protestants, but they are only three out of one hundred of other sorts of Protestants, who all draw their different beliefs from the Bible. Will you, reader, condemn me? If so, tell me how I am to decide, which of these is right, and which wrong? Does the truth of Scripture depend upon the mind of the person who declares it? God has not, nor can He have taught them all differently, unless, as is blasphemy to suppose, He taught them lies, and let them into confusion. Whilst I am thus puzzled, by the good providence of God I suddenly light upon the *original* and *true Church*, from which all these good folks have thought fit to sever themselves, and to become *protesters* against her, even "*the Catholic Church.*" But then, its being the Catholic Church, is quite enough. Truth, I

had been taught to believe, had never been
there; and, indeed, of myself, I should as
soon have thought of going to the moon for it
as to the Catholic Church, *it was so universally
spoken ill of, so universally written against ;*
and more than that, its priests are declared to
be the *worst men alive.*   In fact, if the stories
Protestants tell, and Protestant clergymen too,
were true, the priests could be nothing better
than devils.   This, of course, could not be
the Church of Christ, at least, as I said before,
if all this be true! Blessed be God for this
saving clause, though, at that time, I never
doubted it was true ; but, like all other Protestants, my horror of the Catholic Church
was built upon imaginary evils, flights of my
own fancy, not things that I could either prove
to exist, or prove to be evil.   However, the
question still remained unanswered, where was
the Church of Christ?   I could not tell; however, having by the greatest accident come
across the marks which the Catholic Church
boasts of as a proof that she is the only true
Church pointed out in Scripture, I thought I
would try how far she bore to be compared
with Scripture ; for, that God had pointed out
His own Church in Scripture sufficiently to
direct earnest inquiries, I felt no doubt.

First then, I saw from the whole tenor of
Scripture, as I before explained, the Church

of Christ was to be *one*. The Catholic Church
only I found to be that in all places. Go
where you will, or to what land you like,
there you will find the Catholic Church
identically the same in its doctrine, practices,
and belief, as at the fountain head, Rome, or
elsewhere. Whereas, I saw that to which I
belonged, had come out of the Catholic Church,
and on its new rule of faith had divided itself
into a hundred different beliefs. Besides,
what more common than to hear people talk
thus: "Oh, is not Mr. Blank a beautiful
preacher? I like him because he preaches
High Church." "Oh," says another, "I
like Mr. Suchabody better, because he is Low
Church in his doctrine." Then a third will
say, "I like neither of them so well as some
other Mr.; they don't either of them preach
the Gospel;—but come and hear him, and
for the first time you will hear the truth;"
and so on. But such divisions told me that
the Church to which they belonged could not be
the Church of Christ; for His own words are,
that "no Church or Kingdom divided against
itself can stand;" and most true those words
have proved, as regards the Protestant Church,
for her own people have done more to under-
mine her foundation than even the Catholic
Church, with all her perfections. A second
discovery I made was, that the Church of

Christ should be *evil spoken of*, and that His *true disciples* should be *universally despised;* for when Christ was called *a winebibber*, *a deceiver, and even a devil*, He did not rebuke His slanderers, but mildly turned to His faithful followers, and said: " If they have called Me your Lord and master, all these things, *how much more you; behold this is your heritage?* By this very *reproach, this scorn, these bitter things*, am I at last directed to the true Church of Christ; for who can be at a loss to find out *those men*, whom *all the world*, (who know them not,) *agree in abusing?* None, none, who ever saw a priest of the holy Catholic Church. Oh, yes, happy priests, and holy Church! glory be to God, I have found you both out, for ye are one, and the very things which made me once abhor you both, by the grace of God now lead me to you; and my respect for her sacred priests, set apart for God's service only, is as unbounded now as once it was wanting towards them. Yes, happy priests, those who speak ill of you *must resort to lies;* but let the fulness with which your earthly heritage is heaped upon you be an encouragement and security for that which is to come, and which surely awaits you with increasing brightness, in proportion as your fame in this world is deteriorated. Yes, this is the Church of Christ, this is the faith and the only faith which will sever a child from his parents ; and Christ knew that when He told us. " Ye must not love father and mother more than Me, else ye shall not be worthy of Me;" yes, and this is the faith that even a husband's authority must yield to, and it is that faith for which all must be parted, even the right eye, if required ; and lastly, it is the faith which brings with it a cross to bear by which Jesus marks us for His own. Oh, yes, I have found it at last, and the question which presented itself to me so often as a Protestant, and which I never could answer, is at last answered. The Catholic faith is the faith which will produce these results ; and it is that faith also upon the truth of which a man will willingly stake his immortal soul. Yes, yes, here will I live, and here will I die. I have found a rock, a sure resting-place, a harbour to anchor, where, though varying winds may ruffle, they can never uproot my peace ; and it were as availing to urge a poor weary mariner, who suddenly finds his ship all leaky, her helm gone, and himself unable to stem the tide, to avoid land which he sees within reach, and which offers him shelter and repose, as to try and persuade me to discard this faith.

No, like the mariner, I hear no words, I have no concern but how I can soonest leave the ship that has failed me, to reach the land; and if it were hopeless to urge him before, how still more so when he has reached the land, and finds it offers him a pleasant shade, rich and delicious food, all in fact that his soul could wish for to live and find delight. Would any try and persuade such a one to return to his leaky ship again? then neither need they me, for our cases are similar.

With all these convictions upon my mind, I felt there was but one effort more to be made for the satisfaction of my friends, before I became a Catholic; which was to get a bishop professing each faith to discuss their *rule of faith* before me and other Protestants, to decide which of these men, in equally exalted stations, could prove his church to be founded upon a rock. At this point of my little history, I wrote off to my parents to tell them exactly the state of my mind, and to beg they would send for a sister I had brought with me, for I felt though I might act for myself, I had no right to influence their other child, at least without their knowledge. Having done this, I called upon the Protestant bishop, to make my request to him, but I could not see him as he was from home; however, I wrote to him, to request he would meet the Catholic bishop, to whom I had first made application, and finding *him* ready to do anything to establish my peace and security, I never doubted for a moment I should find my own bishop equally ready.

I was necessitated to make this request of him, because I found that in one conversation with the Catholic bishop, the learning, reading, and result of meditation of my whole life, were uprooted and destroyed. Therefore, I felt the only way to come to a just, fair, and lasting conclusion, was to get my Protestant bishop to defend his and my faith against the Catholic bishop; for although I might not be able to answer all the queries the Protestant bishop might put to me, still I had lost my faith, and the only way it could be restored was to be witness with others to the defeat of the Catholic bishop by the Protestant. This would have satisfied me—nothing short of it could. To this conclusion, I was additionally forced to come by the result of a conversation between the Catholic bishop and my friend the Rev. Mr. H., who suddenly arrived in answer to my letter home, to bear my sister, and myself if he could, from Edinburgh. I, as may well be supposed, refused to return with him, until I proved my own faith, and if I found it fallible, embraced without delay an infallible one, before I dare venture my precious soul on the deep waters.

I urged my friend, therefore, to meet the

7

Catholic bishop, who happened accidentally
to come to the house. He consented. They
talked for about five minutes, and in that
short space of time the bishop had just got
him into a corner, out of which he felt he
never could make an honourable retreat. So,
rising up, he repeated a long passage of
Scripture, with such precision and speed, as
if he thought the feat he had performed was
a silencer in itself, and bounced out of the
room, utterly forgetful of that good breed-
ing which we might expect to find in a
clergyman of so fashionable a Church. The
bishop was actually in the middle of a sen-
tence, when my friend started up. But we
must not be too hard upon him, as it was a
desperate case. I must confess my untutored
temper was not a little tried when, on following him downstairs, I heard him tell my sister it was perfect child's play, talking with
that Catholic bishop! He said so, and although he meant it very differently, I indeed
felt it was but too true to have exposed the
Protestant faith to such a defender, and such
an opponent to the Catholic bishop, who, I
was soon to learn, was the dread and terror
of all the Protestant clergy in Edinburgh.
However, my friend's sudden disappearance
was rather unfortunate at that moment, as
he had just chosen the passage of Scripture

to astonish the bishop with, which his lordship
would have chosen to confound him. Having
this example before me to warn me of the use-
lessness of hearing anything upon the subject of
religion, without witnesses to attest the truth
of what actually passed, I felt little inclined
to meet the Protestant bishop in the way he
wished, to have him say afterwards something in the style of my friend above. Besides, I considered my promise to my parents
to see this bishop quite met, by having conversed with two clergymen on this subject,
since making that promise, and especially as
they both so effectually led me into Catholicity.

The following are my letters to the Protestant bishop, and his replies.

" My lord,
  " The motive which compels me to address your Lordship being one of the utmost
importance, I feel that you will not deem any
apology necessary. Having come to Edinburgh some weeks ago, I have been thrown a
good deal into Catholic society, and doubts
have arisen in my mind with respect to the
grounds of the faith I have sincerely professed during my whole life. I wish some
explanation on this subject, the principal
cause of my uneasiness arising from what

appears to me at present to be the insecure
foundation on which seems to rest the very
essence of my hitherto Protestant convictions.
Will you allow me to ask, if for the sake of
my precious soul, as well as the satisfaction
of my friends, you will be kind enough to
come to my assistance by meeting at Mr.
——, the Rt. Rev. Dr. Gillis, (Catholic
bishop) to discuss with him the rule of faith
Christ must have left to His Church, as upon
the issue of that question must depend my
joining the Catholic Church, or my continued
adherence to the Episcopal communion in
which I was reared.

"Yours, most respectfully,

"FANNY MARIA PITTAR."

: (His Lordship's reply.)

"Madam,

"I lose no time in answering your
note, and in assuring you, *that I am anxious
to do anything in my power for bringing your
mind to a steady conviction of the true faith*,
as delivered to mankind by Christ and His
apostles. But you must allow me to doubt
whether the most rational plan for this purpose is for me to meet and discuss the rule
of faith with Dr. Gillis, in your presence.

"From such a conference you might have
sufficient grounds for deciding which was the

cleverer man, which had studied the subject most carefully, and other points entirely personal to the two disputants, but very remotely bearing upon the great point at issue.

"It appears to me much more expedient that I should, at any rate in the first instance, see you alone, and know, from your own explanation, what are the points in which the creed in which you have been educated, appears to you unsatisfactory, and wherein the Romish Church appears to offer you greater satisfaction.

"I will, if you choose, call for you on Monday, between one and two o'clock. In the meantime, earnestly advising you to lay all your doubts before Him, who has promised that those who will do His will shall know of the doctrine, whether it be of God or of men,

"I am, Madam,

"Yours faithfully,

"C. H. S. Bishop."

(My second Letter.)

"My Lord,

"In reply to your note of yesterday, I beg to say that my reason for requesting the conference between you and Dr. Gillis was more for the sake of showing to my friends I had not refused to hear both sides of the question fairly argued, than for the satis-

faction of my own mind. I therefore applied
to your Lordship as the highest authority of
that light I had hitherto followed, and wished
to listen to what Dr. Gillis, the authority on
the other side, would say, in opposing to you
the rule of faith of the Church to which he
belongs, and which lays claim to an unbroken
line of succession from the Apostles, and also
to the inheritance of the promises of Jesus
Christ, to be with her all days, even to the
end of the world.

"Your objecting to such a conference, as
affording grounds of contrast to the abilities of
the disputants, would be equally met by separate interviews. I feel then, that the benefit
you would derive for me shall be best, and
indeed I may say, can only be obtained were
I and an unprejudiced friend to be present at
what you and Bishop Gillis would say for your
respective communions.

"If your Lordship decline this, my conscience is clear. I shall forward to my relations your reasons for so doing, along with
my own for declining private conference.
But if your Lordship will meet me to-morrow,
to discuss with Dr. Gillis, very briefly, the
comparative rules of faith of the two Churches,
it would be a great favour.

"Most respectfully yours,
"FANNY MARIA PITTAR."

" Madam,

"I still think that the result of a conference between me and Bishop Gillis, in your presence, would be nothing better than a determination whether Dr. Gillis or I were the acuter disputant. By private interviews, on the other hand, leading to the requisite reading on the subject, you would learn, not what we can say in a given time, but what can be said on both sides of the subject.

"The questions at issue between us of the *Reformed Catholic Church* and those who adhere to the communion of Rome, are so numerous and may be treated in such various ways, that, unless I knew something beforehand of your state of information and convictions, my arguments might be quite beside the purpose.

"Of course this objection would be strengthened if I thought that Dr. Gillis had personally or by information a knowledge of your present views, respecting which I am entirely in the dark.

"While then, madam, I offer to visit you, as a minister of Christ, and to counsel you to the best of my knowledge, I must still decline meeting Bishop Gillis, for whose character and attainments, it is right to say, I feel a high respect.

> "I am, Madam,
> "Your obedient Servant,
> "C. H. S. Bishop."

(My Reply.)

"My Lord,

"In reply to your note of last evening, I beg to say most respectfully, I am quite satisfied. What I asked of your Lordship was, not to prove the state of my mind, but whether the Protestant rule of faith was infallible or not. Your declining to meet Dr. Gillis to discuss this subject, only strengthens me in my new but present faith. He did not desire this meeting, but I asked it of him to enable me to decide.

"If then Bishop Gillis, to win a soul, would do most gladly what you cannot bring yourself to, to save one, I with a heart overpowered with gratitude to God for showing me at last where truth is, if I had not abundant other proofs, should now embrace Catholicity, from the different spirit, I am forced to conclude, guides and influences her different bishops.

> "Yours respectfully,
> "FANNY MARIA PITTAR."

The above letters I should not feel myself at liberty to make public, had they been written under the badge of friendship: they were not so. I addressed his lordship, as the head of the Protestant Church in Edinburgh, as the shepherd I was to apply to for succour, but I fled to him in vain; therefore, I count he can be but an hireling, when he would not make a sacrifice to save one of his flock.

The result of my communication with the Protestant bishop, I have given, and I confess, by the time it was over, I felt little inclined to go and learn my catechism again, as he would fain think necessary. I thought twenty-eight years quite enough to have devoted to it already, along with Protestant preaching and reading, to which I devoted myself, especially for the last twelve years, with great sincerity, caring for nothing else; and if it was to stand me in no better stead, than that a few conversations with a Catholic was to overturn it all, I felt, as I said before, little inclined to trust myself to its guidance again. Indeed I felt persuaded that a person who began to see her own faith and Church to be false, and another right, and who, to be guided and directed, still went to the ministers of her former Church, acted no wiser a part than one, who found suddenly she had been drinking poison, when, instead of *instantly having recourse to an antidote*, she said, as the poison was sweet, I will have a little more first. The one would have as good a chance to be saved as the other;—so I thought at least, and therefore I acted up to my convictions.

But, although the Protestant bishop would not come to my help, or rather, would not expose himself to the power of truth (for if he possessed it himself, what need he have cared to face all the talents ever heaped upon man) I felt a great desire, knowing the effect truth had upon myself, that some of these good and sincere Protestant clergymen should be induced, under the plea for my sake (but entirely for their own), to meet this so much dreaded Catholic bishop. Just at this time, a good and pious Presbyterian lady, who felt truly concerned at my change, (she being the sister of my friend's husband,) and who, on discovering my religious tendency, had fain hoped I should have convinced her sister-in-law of the errors of Catholicity, instead of being myself convinced of its truth, gave me the opportunity of doing my best to attain this end, by herself proposing there should be a meeting of clergymen holding different faiths. She herself said she would be quite delighted to be present.

I then told her I could get no clergyman to

meet a Catholic priest, but that any or all of
the priests were ready at a call.

ᵖ At hearing this her indignation arose, and
she started off, saying *she* would find plenty,
who would be only too glad to come—-men
whose zeal for the salvation of souls was such,
that they would snatch with delight any
opportunity of rescuing one from destruction;
and she ended by saying, "If your clever
Episcopalians will not come, you shall see
what Presbyterian clergy are made of." She
went away, and in all anxiety, I waited her
returning, hoping to have to tell the bishop I
had some scores of Protestant *divines* to meet
him; but lo! instead of herself and the clergymen, a note came to say, her clergy could not
have a *private interview* with a Catholic
clergyman, FOR FEAR OF DISSENTION! but that
they would meet Dr. Gillis on *a public platform.* To the above I made the following
reply—the proposal which I was authorised to
make by this good and zealous man, who
shrank not to declare his Master's truth and
cause in any way, or every way wherein he
could hope for His blessing.

" MY DEAR MISS,
    "I deeply regret on your account, as you
expressed so strong a desire to hear both sides
of this question, that these *zealous gentlemen* to

whom you have been, cannot venture, *even to save a soul*, on a *private interview*. In my humble opinion, a private discussion is less likely to breed dissension than a public one. Their *very generous* offer to come forward publicly, I must inform you, has not so much in it as you may suppose, as they must all be aware, that Bishop Gillis has *publicly* and in *print* stated, that he would meet any individual or number of clergymen in any way, *except on a public platform!* His reasons for refusing this are many and good; however, for your sake he is willing to do much, and therefore he authorizes me to say he will meet any number of clergymen you can collect, or that your brother's drawing-rooms will hold, which will not be less than 200, and he will not require one Catholic to support, or be present with him.

" If I seem over anxious on this subject, you must forgive me ; it is because I have seen in you a sincerity and desire, which possessing myself, I have been unable to resist Catholicity. But I would just remark, that although I hold every doctrine and principle of the Catholic Church, as Catholics hold them, yet not one as Protestants conceive them. Believe there is something in all this, something worth your attention; and as a lie will always discover upon itself, surely a person professing (as they suppose) the truth, need not be afraid to make the search.

" Most sincerely yours,

"FANNY MARIA PITTAR."

To the above letter I received another negative. These very conscientious gentlemen would not meet Dr. Gillis—they must beg to decline doing so, since *he could only declare the truth in a corner!* that corner, however, would have held more than all the Protestant clergymen in Edinburgh. *But any excuse is better than to face the truth, when one is not prepared to embrace it!*

When I had reached this point, I could not but feel I had done enough to satisfy any reasonable being of my sincerity, and therefore I determined to trifle no longer with the grace that was given me. On the 24th of February, 1842, *I became a Catholic!* an undeserving, but a happy Catholic, my peace increasing with my days!

A Catholic! I a Catholic! the thought is startling, and the idea almost overwhelming! but lest my feelings should be misconceived, let me pause one moment in my little narrative, to indulge in the delicious thought; and whilst I think, oh! how shall I refrain from that power divine by which I know and feel

this wonderful change has been wrought in me.
Once so zealously and sincerely opposed to
everything Catholic, *now*, as it were, living
and feeding upon it, to my soul's unspeakable
delight. Once a respected member of a respected society, a devoted child to the best of
parents, a beloved wife of an incomparable
husband, a doating mother of a lively offspring,
now, severed perhaps in every one of the above
relations, and yet *resigned, contented, possessing only Catholicity !* Oh, mystery worthy of
being solved, how shall I endeavour to unfold
the secret, which God Himself could only have
revealed to me !

Need I here increase my own deep feeling
of what I owe to God, for this wonder He has
wrought in me, or the amazement of those who
may, with unbiassed feelings, trace the path I
have lately trodden, by recalling or adverting
to the appeals made to me by those I almost
held dearer than life, at that trying moment
when first the thought, the immense thought,
forced itself upon me, that the Catholic Church
was the true and only Church of Christ, and
that if I would save my immortal soul, I must
enter its fold, even at the loss of all those dear
ties? Need I revert to the heart-rending
appeals made to me by a mother whom I
adored, and to whom, till now, I had ever been
a consolation, not to break her heart, not to

inflict the severest pang she had ever felt, by
taking the dreadful step of declaring myself a
Catholic; or first to the importunity, prayers,
arguments, entreaties, and then threats of a
father whom I had never before offended?
Or, need I hint at the thousand hopes and
fears which alternately rushed upon me, as to
the effect the news might have upon my
absent husband, whose love and fidelity,
though I had once thought them stronger than
death, I now almost fancied might yield?
Need I revert to all this, and a thousand other
real and imaginary woes, which rent and tore
my heart, until then, almost a stranger to real
sorrow?   Yes, I will just allude to them,
(paint them as they really were, I never can),
that should these lines meet the eye of any
one, who, like myself, was reared in ignorance
of that truth by which only the soul may be
assured of happiness, yet still possessing that
sincerity for his salvation, as to enable him
even to part with *all* for its sake, he may see I
did not embrace Catholicity without a struggle, and keen and sharp as that struggle was,
he may know still further that it was worth
enduring, yes, if it could have been ten thousand times more acute than it was, for the
treasure I know and feel I possess in consequence.   Oh, let me close my eyes to the
dark side of this little sketch, and paint for a

minute the peace, the calm, the security, the delight, the ecstasy of having come to truth, truth that can never fail, truth that will be the same when all that now exists shall have passed away for ever,—and that truth, too, revealing, bestowing, and manifesting to me Jesus Christ, the Redeemer of my soul, who said: " I will show you what great things you must suffer for My sake;" and again, " If ye love *father, mother, husband, or children* more than Me, ye are not worthy of Me." Yes, it was for Jesus I endured all, and did He leave me without a recompense? Oh! let my tongue be sealed in death when it shall cease to praise Him for the mercy He has shown me, for the recompense He has heaped upon me, for the peace I enjoy, for all and everything. Even my very sorrows—I can but praise Him for them, for they led me to joys unknown and untasted, but by those for whom they are prepared.

The step taken, my peace made with heaven, and my soul enjoying the precious fruits of the happy exchange I had made, my thoughts naturally fell upon the good man who had first been the means of leading me to suspect all was not right with the foundation on which I had been building for eternity.

His answer relative to Ash Wednesday,

showed me he was not perfectly satisfied with what he professed himself. Instantly, therefore, I determined to go to him, and tell him all that had happened to me, if, perhaps, God might thereby convince him it was better to sell all in this world, to buy eternal life in the next. I went to him—we conversed for more than two hours. I told him how happy I was, and how infinitely I preferred the scorn and desertion of the world, with what I possessed, to the whole world without it. He looked quite puzzled, and said nothing, but that I had taken a very awful step. I asked him if he would read something I would give him, because I persisted in asserting he did not know what the Catholic faith was. He said he would read anything I gave him. I told him I had done my best to get *his* bishop to meet the Catholic one, before I became a Catholic, but that he would not do so. He said, if it was not treason (these were his very words) to say so, he thought his bishop had done very wrong, but that if I had gone to him before I became a Catholic, he certainly would have *done anything to save me;* for he thought I had done an awful thing, and he pitied me from his soul, being so misled. This was all very good, and natural, but now for the proof of his sincerity. "Will you," said I, "come and meet my bishop, and prove your rule of faith before him ?" "No," said he, "certainly not; you are past hope, therefore, why should I do so useless a thing? Had you applied to me in time to save your soul, I would have done that, or anything else, but not now." Why I did not apply to him was, I thought my friend Miss —— had done so, for I knew he was a favourite of hers, although not belonging to the same form of worship, and although I do not know positively whether she did or not—I really believe she did, but that is nothing to the present purpose. Well, said I, that is just and fair, but one soul is just of as much value to you as another, especially as I never saw you before, but once in my life, and never may again. I come to you, therefore, in behalf of another, who has witnessed my conversion, who sees that I have failed to get any Protestant clergyman to meet a Catholic one, or to defend his faith; will you come, therefore, for the sake of this person, who is no other than the husband of my dear friend, and who, I have every reason to believe and hope, will very soon follow my example, simply because he sees you are all afraid to defend the faith you profess.

After some hesitation, he said: "I do not think I am called upon to do so, for Mr. ——, for *if I did*, I should be called upon by Mr. A——, and Mr. B——, and Mr. C——, and

thus I should be taken up instead of attending
to my own people, to whom l owe more than
I can even accomplish." I here urged his
inconsistency, and demanded if it did not
strike him there was something the matter
when no Protestant clergyman would dare to
face a Catholic priest. "Oh," said he, "it
is exposing our truth, for we all know what
a clever man Dr. Gillis is." But said I, all
the talents in the world can never *prove* a lie
to be *truth ;* no, you know it cannot, therefore come, in the name of God, if you think
you possess truth, and the moment you confound my Catholic clergyman, I cease to
be a Catholic. I was very earnest indeed,
for I hoped the man was sincere ; and I felt
if I could only get him to come, his own eyes
might be opened. I did not therefore stand
upon any ceremony, and my importunity was
so great, that he was *constrained to meet me
half way.* "I will tell you then," said he,
"what I will do for you. I will hear Dr.
Gillis discuss with you the rule of faith, and
I will go behind a screen, and when *he is gone
I will prove* all he said to be false!!!" Mr.
D——, you astonish me, I am utterly amazed,
and can hardly believe my own ears ; said I,
and can only say, I regret, indeed, that no one
is present, but these walls, to witness to your
words.

Whoever reads this, need not be surprised
I did not give him the opportunity of giving
me this proof! We parted.—My feeling of
sorrow for him being much greater and better
founded than his for me. But I did not give
him up. I knew him to be a good though
deceived man, and I still hoped. I believe he
was perfectly puzzled at my earnestness, for
he promised to read two tracts for me.

Some days after I felt anxious to know the
result upon his mind of the perusal of my
pamphlets. I went, therefore, to him again,
and conversed for another two hours. To the
best of my tracts, "The Church of Peace
and Truth," he had nothing whatever to object,
except that there were some quotations from
Scripture in it which he did not think
applicable. But in the other, he said there
was a horrid blasphemy, which was quite
sufficient for him, and that was, the Blessed
Virgin being styled "The Mother of God."
I was so surprised at his denying this, that I
could say nothing, for I thought we must
have misunderstood each other. So I left
him still begging, as a great favour, he would
read Dr. Wiseman's lectures on Transubstantiation, as he objected much to that doctrine.
He said he would. However, when I got
home I thought over all we had said, and all
I might have said; and I thought I would

make one trial more, by writing the following letter:—

"DEAR SIR,

"Once more I intrude myself upon your notice, humbly hoping that the sincerity you have witnessed in me will plead an excuse to you in my behalf, for such intrusions. ˙ Oh, why is it that I am so anxious, so solicitous about you? why, but because, by the providence of God, I was directed to you when a stranger in a strange land, as His minister, and one on whom I felt I had a claim as such to solve a difficulty. Your reply was such as to prove to me I was on an insecure foundation for my immortal soul, and that you were not yourself *perfectly satisfied* with *every* appointment of your own Church. From thence, as also afterwards from your own mouth, I learned that although you feel quite calm, you feel quite certain you have found a Saviour able and willing to save your soul; still you will till death fear and tremble, feeling it not impossible your rule of faith may be fallible, and therefore, not such as will stand you at the awful day of judgment. This then, along with the universal voice, pronouncing you a sincere and godly man, makes me feel interested for you beyond what words can express.

"But why, again, should this interest be excited towards one who professes himself satisfied with the faith he holds, although he cannot prove it infallible? why, but because (if I would not be misunderstood as comparing myself, who am less than the very least, to one so capable, so learned, and so devoted as yourself), it is but one short month since I held with powerful sincerity the very same faith you, this instant, rest upon; yes, and I held it zealously. Nevertheless, within that short space of time, it has pleased God to show me a more perfect, more united, and a better rule of faith; one worthy of God, *because infallible*—a way so straight, that the eye can see with clearness even to the very end of it; so garnished with truth and certainty, that the soul let into it from a bye-path, on first finding it, is so overwhelmed with joy and gratitude that in telling others of the way she has found, they can but suspect her of madness; so great is her delight, for it is a way so simple and safe that the way-faring man, though a fool, cannot err therein—a way in which all are invited to go, and from which none are excluded but those who will not try for themselves, whether it be all, it is so joyously and fearlessly declared to be by those who have already tried it.

"Twice I have had the privilege of conversing

with you since this happy change in my faith.
On these occasions, nothing passed from you
to shake my present views—much to strengthen
them.   You will, perhaps, start at this, remembering the isolated passages of Scripture
you brought forward, supposing them capable
of overturning doctrines founded on the whole
tenor of Scripture.   But I shall not detain
you to speak on this subject, but bear with me
while I remark upon the expression you used
as referring to the Blessed Virgin being called
in a Catholic book ' the Mother of God.'   It
was, you said, *blasphemous.*   At the moment
you made use of the expression, I was so
utterly astonished at such a term being applied
to such a subject by a Bible clergyman, I
really forgot everything in a feeling of deep
humility and gratitude, that to me such blessed
realities should ever have been revealed ;
while the wise, and the great, and sometimes
the good (for you are a good man, and too
good a one to remain in a faith that cannot
be maintained and proved before the learned
and the unlearned, the talented and ignorant)
are left uncalled.

   " What can I do for you?   One thing I
have in my power, and cannot be prevented
using it ; I can pray for you, and I will.   But
may I beg of you to open your Bible, which,
you profess, directs you, and from which you

declare your rule of faith to be drawn, doing
all it commands, and refraining from all it
forbids, and tell me if the following passages
do not declare Mary ever blessed to be the
Mother of God : Isaiah vii. 14, ix. 6 ; Matt.
i. 18, 20, 23 ; Luke i. 35, 42, 43, 44, 45, 48,
xxviii. 37 ; Acts i. 14, xx. 28. If they do
not, then as a Protestant I could but despair,
since my very mother tongue must be re-
studied to enable me rightly to understand
this rule of faith, which according to my present
knowledge of English, leads me to a directly
opposite view to yours. So, what is to be
done? What Protestant can hope for heaven,
if to get there it be necessary to live up to
their rule of faith, and yet the talent necessary
to understand it aright is such, that even their
own ministers cannot trust themselves to speak
or declare their rule to one of a different faith?
Oh! what, tell me, is to become of the ignorant
and unlearned? must they all perish? No,
no; let them come into that Church which has
a rule adapted to all capacities and understand-
ings, and in doing so they will do well, for it
will be the faith God Himself intended for
them, as God, in justice, could never have
sent a rule of faith so difficult to be understood,
and *so incapable of being defended and proved.*
Indeed, my dear sir, I cannot but wonder how
it is possible to raise a doubt as to the propriety

of calling the Blessed Virgin ' Mother of God,' for if our Lord Jesus Christ be God, as I conceive is clearly stated above, how can the Blessed Virgin be anything but Mother of God? This is the faith the apostles taught us, although they made not use of the word. But you will say, perhaps, is Mary then the mother of the Deity? My answer is, that being Mother of the Man who was united to the Eternal Word, so as to form one person, she ought to be called the Mother of God, though not the Mother of the Deity. Besides, all Protestants acknowledge the four first Councils of the Church, and at the third, at Ephesus, Nestorius, a bishop, was excommunicated for exactly saying as you do, that Mary was not Mother of God. You will find the above remarks in St. Cyril's writings in Butler's Lives of the Saints, which fell under my notice since I last saw you. I am sure I need not try further to prove my sincerity, but would to God you would inwardly resolve to investigate this matter, yes, even at all hazards —your reward would be great. More I cannot therefore do than pray for you, which I do in all sincerity.

" Yours,

"FANNY MARIA PITTAR."

(His reply.)

"DEAR MADAM,

" An unusual pressure of urgent duties has prevented me from answering your letter before now, and even now my reply must be brief.

"You are entirely mistaken in supposing that I feel a moment's doubt or hesitation respecting the infallibility of the rule of faith on which I rest, and your misapprehensions in this respect, notwithstanding the repeated declarations I have made to you on the subject, prove to me how correct I have been in resolving not to discuss the matter before you—prove indeed, how absurd it would have been for me to have entertained the proposal for a moment.* The texts you adduce respecting the expression, 'Mother of God,' you must allow me to say, are completely wide of the mark ; they tend to prove the divinity of Christ, which doctrine I hold, but they leave the expression entirely unsupported, and I therefore repeat what I said before, that it is *unscriptural* as well as *unreasonable, blasphemous* as well as *false.*

---

* Strange, if I was so much mistaken, that in less than nine months after the date of this letter, this worthy gentleman should have dissented from the Church, forsaken his parish and flock, to become a Nonintrusionist.

"I beg to return Wiseman's book, which I have read. It bears the stamp of the writer's mind, learning, ingenuity, and plausibility ; but sooner might you build a castle on a cob-web, than the doctrine of transubstantiation upon his argument. In spite of his talent and his special pleadings, the doctrine hangs like a millstone about his neck, heavy in its iniquity, dishonouring to God, idolatrous in its practice, and ruinous in its consequences. I beg you to excuse this short reply to your long letter : but you must, I think, be aware that all which appears so new and attractive and convincing to you, is neither one nor the other to me; and you ought not to expect me to give the time to write out formal refutations of errors, which have been repeatedly and fully exposed from the press. I cannot do more than express the bitterness of sorrow that I feel for the fatal step you have taken, and my earnest prayer that you may yet be recovered out of the snare which has been laid for you.

"Your's very truly,

"D. T. K. D."

Need I produce more facts, to excuse myself to those of my family who may read what I have here stated? Will any condemn me for the choice I have made? My case stands

thus : I find my soul in danger ; I first apply
to a bishop of my former church to come forward and save it, at the same time pointing
out the danger and the enemy that threatened
it ; but he says, " No, *I cannot face the enemy
openly*—I must know your mind first, for fear
I should fight with weapons *unsuitable and un-
available !*" Then I try a second—a man
with less policy, but more courage, than the
prudent bishop, and he says, " Oh, yes ; I will
meet this dreadful man;" but before they are
five minutes together, he acts on the principle
of a good retreat being better than a bad
stand, and up he starts, and runs out of the
room.

Then others, I am told, are ready to come
to my succour ; but when the danger draws
near, they urge they cannot come *privately,
for fear of dissension*, but they would come
publicly and openly, by which they knew, if
they had not the advantage in argument, they
would at least in numbers, as all there dissent
from the enemy they dared not meet. And
lastly, another offers his assistance, because he
could not resist my importunity, but it *must be
behind a screen !*

All this, on the one hand, whereas on the
other I find the greatest readiness to do everything or anything that my soul requires to
make it at peace with its Maker. The true

Shepherd says, " Yes, I will brave danger for
even one of my Master's sheep, even to the
loss of all things ; for life, to me, is only worth
having, as I can make it the means of succour-
ing and protecting those over whom I have
been appointed a shepherd."—I have made
my choice, and those who will condemn me,
must.

More reasons I could give for this great, this
glorious change, yes, this happy, this peaceful
change.   Many more, indeed, I could give,
but will the patience of the reader bear with
me in an addition so unnecessary ?   Will not
every candid, unprejudiced heart, with one
spark of sincerity or truth in its composition,
pronounce me guiltless?   To have resisted
would have been to have fought against God,
and though most unworthy of the great honour
of being called to bear a reproached name for
Christ's sake, nevertheless the grace has been
given me, and I must declare it, though with
fear and trembling, lest, as He has not spared
some of the natural branches, so He might
not spare me, an ingrafted one.   But through
the power of that *daily food* prepared for my
soul, I will hope unto the end.   I am happy,
more than happy.   I have obtained a possession for myself, and an inheritance for my
children, as rich as it was unexpected, as satisfactory as it is secure.

My Bible is now a treasure to me beyond all price; it led me to Catholicity, and as a Catholic I can render it the honour due to it. To me it is infallible, because I have it from an infallible Church. No more to me belongs the prerogative of hearing my preacher to condemn him. I know, if he holds not truth, he never could be in the place where my instructor stands. And my Bible is to me like a beautiful picture, reflecting some renowned artist's sublime imagination. I can contemplate the light and shade with rapture, as long as I have them as He left them, but let some presumptuous student bedaub it with his unskilful touches, and I turn with disgust and dissatisfaction from what was, originally, instructive as beautiful.

After feasting my soul till Easter week in the dear land of my soul's birth, I returned to Dublin, but not to the happy home, nor to the embrace of those dear ones whom I had so lately left. A mother's love had weathered the storm—she came to meet me, but her love was changed. She came to mourn over her disgraced child—she came to conduct me to cold and lonely lodgings, and to break to me the news that I rendered myself unfit longer to be the guardian or protectress of my children, and that those children could no longer gladden my heart with their presence, at least, not

until their father's wishes were known upon
the subject. She came, in short, to mingle
her tears with mine—to mourn over the wreck
I was reduced to, but to avert which I had no
power. But let me pass over this moment of
agony—this moment in which nature was tried
to its extent, but over which grace had a
glorious and complete victory. However, to
prove my case still further, I shall copy a
letter I had occasion to write to the Rev. J.
G—g, a *great star!* before whom my beloved
and well-intentioned father insisted I should
come, to be shown the fallacy of all my new
notions. As this great man, by his own
account, was about to turn the whole Catholic
world Protestants, he was, in consequence, just
the man to annihilate me. I cannot refrain
from giving this letter, because by it will be
seen what passed between us, and an additional
instance given of the instability and uncertainty
of the Protestant faith, and of the insufficiency
of Protestant argument. My dear father was
present during this meeting, and as I felt over
anxious on his account as to the defence I
should make, I in consequence omitted some
things, which I could not rest till I had repaired
by the following letter :—

"Rev. Sir,

"It is not when most depends upon our words that we are always able to choose the best. The very importance we attach to our defence, when arraigned before a judge, incapacitates us for making a good one; hence it is, that the laws of our country have provided for persons so situated.

"It was something of this kind prevented me, when brought up before you to give a reason for my change of faith, from saying much, that under other circumstances I should have said. I felt most deeply both for yourself and my beloved parent, who was by knowing that God could if it pleased Him, through my words, remove the film from both your eyes which has been strengthening with your strength, and forming since your birth. I felt, in short, *over anxious*, forgetting that my own inability and utter unworthiness would but tend to God's greater glory.

"The defence, therefore, which I could have made, I was incapable of doing through my human frailty and want of faith in God.

"During that meeting, you reminded me that I should have to account before God for every word that passed between us. This truth had caused me many prayers previous to seeing you, and now urges me to make this effort, to endeavour to repair what I then left unsaid; for I feel, I at least was unfaithful to the trust committed to me, and the opportunity offered of declaring God's truth. Bear with me, therefore, dear Sir, and believe me I am most sincere; and pardon the apparent presumption of my supposing that I, who am so ignorant and incapable, could direct you who are so learned. Bear with me, I ask again, because I am sincere; and remember my presumption springs from the thoughts that not many *wise*, not many *learned*, are called; but the *foolish* and the *base* of this world, and those that are *not* to bring to nought those that *are*. With the timidity, therefore, of the little maid, who venturing her simple appeal to a great king, was made the means of great results, do I hope to bear a message to you, Sir, and to tell you the argument you held against me proved your faith unsound, and not according to Scripture.

"Your first assertion against me was, that in becoming a Catholic, I had forsaken my reason, my senses, and my Bible. Whatever answer I made you to this, I beg now to say my reason, such as it is, led me to become a Catholic. Born and reared a Protestant, I should ever have remained such, had it not been for the good Providence of God who

9

directed me to one who inquired of me why
and against what I was protesting. I said
"the errors of Popery," (the same I suppose
that you termed their weak point, and upon
which you assured my father you were so capable
of attacking them.)   I was naturally requested
to name them.   I did do so, one after the other.
To many of my charges I was answered,
'They were not Catholic doctrines at all, only
Protestant conception of them.'   The rest
were proved to me to be Scriptural. It now
became my turn to inquire what Catholic
doctrine really was, for I found out I knew
nothing of it, and I confess I had the sincerity
about me to believe the faith I had would
stand *any test* ; otherwise, reason told me it
could not be from God, and if not, the sooner
I changed it the better, no matter what the
results.   When I heard what the Catholic
faith really was, I was compelled to assent to
its being most reasonable. That faith has
existed unaltered through all generations, the
chain reaches unbroken from Christ to the
present hour ; whereas, the Protestant faith
I knew to have sprung out of the reformation
(falsely so called) commenced by Luther, who
has himself left on record that in his religious
opinions, *he stood alone* in the world ; therefore, my reason told me that the faith which
commenced three hundred years ago, could

not be the faith which Jesus Christ had left
us eighteen hundred years ago.   I also knew
from history that the Protestant articles of
belief were in the reign of Henry VIII. but
six ; that afterwards, in the reign of Edward
VI., they were changed to *forty-two;* and
lastly, that in Elizabeth's day, they were, as
now, *thirty-nine.*   My *reason* told me all this
was not of God.   Therefore by my *reason,* so
far, I became a Catholic.   Blame the reason
if you like, that is quite another point; but
such as it was, it was it that led me into
Catholicity.

" My   dear   sir,   try   and   forget   for   one
moment, that word so horrible to Protestants,
' Catholics,' and also the creature who addresses
you ; and ask yourself what it was Christ
promised His disciples as the head of His
Church.   He promised them His Holy Spirit,
and that Holy Spirit should guide them to all
truth, and if He did guide them into all truth,
and if they fell from it afterwards as you say,
what becomes of the second part of His
promise that He would be with them all days,
even to the end of the world?   What was the
use of sending truth to the disciples to benefit
all the world, if those that followed were to
forsake and fall from it?   No, no, Sir ; the
Scripture abounds with promises to Christ's
Church, that once He gave Himself for the

redemption of man, He would never forsake
His ·Church or people afterwards. He also
has said, that His Church shall be without
spot or wrinkle, and that in it there should be
but *one Lord, one faith,* and *one baptism, one
fold;* and let me ask you, sir, where is the
oneness of anything Protestant? We hear
of such a Protestant minister being so
celebrated, but is it not, I ask you, honestly,
the next question, *what doctrine does he preach?*
The Bible, I say, is replete with promises to
the Church of God. Look to Isaiah liv.,
indeed the whole of Isaiah. And what does
Christ say in the New Testament? 'Whoso-
ever hears you, hears Me; and whoseever
rejects you, rejects Me. For I will never
leave you, nor forsake you, I will be with you
always, even to the end of the world.' Think
of all this, dear Sir, and tell me, did Christ
forsake His Church from the sixth to the
fifteenth century, as Protestants say? Oh,
surely not, when He said He never would.
Think not, because I say as Christ said, there
should be but *one fold,* that I exclude any.
No; if a Catholic rejoices at his being in this
fold, he never forgets that Christ also said,
'He had sheep of another fold, which He
would also bring.' The silent prayer, therefore,
of every good and sincere Catholic is, that
each dear friend and relative in the Pro-

testant faith may be of that fold, and may
yet be brought into it. Such, my dear Sir,
though you may not be able to appreciate it,
is my earnest prayer for you and others.

" Your next point against me was, that I
had forsaken my senses. So far from having
forsaken them, I find them all called into
daily exercise *now*, whereas, as a Protestant,
as far as religion was concerned, I never used
them at all. I now see the beauty of truth,
I now *feel* the benefits resulting from it, I now
hear the gospel promises, I now have a foretaste of their fulfilment, and lastly, I have a
sweet smelling savour of what shall be given both
here and hereafter to those who remain firm
until death to the measure of grace delivered
to them; whereas, as a Protestant, I knew
the truth was beautiful, but I could not see it;
I therefore prayed hard that I might, and God
has more than answered me. I did not feel
the benefit of the truth, but I prayed that I
might, and God has in this also heard me;
for now that I possess it, I not only know it but
am satisfied to the full. I heard the Gospel
it is true, but in such a variety of forms and
shapes, that I was unable to decide which was
the perfection of truth until I had recourse to
my stronghold, 'prayer,' to be directed which
to choose; and I have been at last enabled to
decide. I had also a foretaste, but it was

only that óne day`I should possess what *I now enjóy*, and a sweet smelling savour of what my soul is now inhaliug to its unspeakable joy and peace.

"The third and last point was my Bible, that I had forsaken it. Now we will suppose for one minute that I have, am I worse off than the thousands who Jived and died for the first ninety-six years after Christ's death? There was no Bible then at all. But I will go even further, and ask now, am I worse off than the myriads and myriads who lived and died for the first 1500 years after Christ? There was as good as no Bible then. Were all these souls lost then for want of a Bible? If not, then I hope to be saved as they were. But I will not allow I have forsaken my Bible, for I know and feel it is only now I can truly appreciate it.

"Speaking of the Blessed Sacrament being really the body and blood of Christ, as Catholics believe it, you first asserted there was not one passage in Scripture to warrant such a supposition, and next, that it was *contrary to reason*.

"Now as to the first, I asked you, was it a point conceded that I understood English? You did me the favour to suppose it. I then referred you to the sixth chapter of St. John, where Christ declares *this mystery*. The disciples and the Jews who were by, said, *But how,* for like you, Sir, they understood Him literally, and thought it contrary to reason. However, our blessed Saviour, instead of enlightening them, which surely He would if the case would have admitted of it, simply answers them, 'I tell you, upon oath, VERILY, VERILY, IT IS MY FLESH, and unless *ye eat of it,* ye shall have no life in you.' And again, for fear there should be any misconception about it, as He had chosen that substance to convey Himself to the world, He goes on to say, *he that eats Me* even he shall live by *Me.* At this, even His very disciples murmured, and some forsook Him for the saying; but He merely said to them, 'does this offend you, if so, how much more will ye be offended when ye see Me rise whole and entire to My Father in heaven?' Oh, Sir, I ask you, would not our Saviour have explained, if He could, to have saved those who forsook Him? but no, He does it not.   When I had finished, you very quietly told me I had made a great mistake, for that chapter did not apply to the Sacrament of the Lord's Supper at all. This was something quite new: however, I turned to the eleventh chapter of 1 Cor. 29th verse, where it says, they who communicate unworthily, eat and drink their own damnation, NOT DISCERNING THE LORD'S BODY.   I asked you if this referred

to the Sacrament, to which you instantly
replied, Yes; then I refer to the marginal
reference of my Oxford Bible, and it refers
me from that passage to the sixth chapter of
John. Now, sir, I ask you, is it likely God
would damn us for not discerning what by
your account is not to be discerned? or what
am I or any Protestant to do? We are told
to examine our Bible, and compare Scripture
with Scripture, and either my Bible has led
me astray, or you are under a mistake.
Which it must be, I leave you to decide.

"Having gained this advantage over you,
you instantly changed the subject, and urged
the unreasonableness of the doctrine of transubstantiation. It was contrary, you insisted
to reason, for indeed, neither reason nor sense
will permit us to believe such a doctrine.
But that you, a Bible clergyman, should condemn my belief on such grounds not a little
surprises me; and indeed I am sure any
candid person would allow such an unexpected
charge was enough to put me off my defence.

"I now beg to tell you, sir, it is not by
reason nor by sense my Catholic hopes are
to be saved, but by *faith*, and that transubstantiation is above both, I allow, but not
more so than the *Incarnation of our Lord*. I
remember I said this to you, and you answered,
'Yes, but we saw our Lord.' Now, although

I cannot exactly agree with you there, for I never saw Him, yet I will suppose the case that you did see Him; Christ says, 'Blessed are they who not having seen, shall believe.' Besides, supposing you did see Him, it was only the man Jesus you saw; but of what avail would believing in Christ's manhood be, unless you added His Godhead also? Is it therefore according to reason, I would ask you, that God was born man *in a stable, of a Virgin, and suffered death to redeem man?* If it be, your reasoning powers must differ from all your fellow men; if it is not, then you believe it not according to reason, or what is still more probable, not believe it at all.

"But I would ask you once more, is the doctrine of the Blessed Trinity according to reason? I am sure you cannot say yes, and yet, I know, you dare not say you do not believe it. It cannot be that you will say, as in the case of Christ, that you have seen the Blessed Trinity. Do you, Sir, believe this doctrine? If so, it is not according to reason you believe—thousands, I know, think it contrary to reason, but they are consistent for holding your argument; they reject it from their creed for its unreasonableness. It therefore follows, either you are inconsistent, or you believe not according to reason. I would also ask you, if reason were our only rule in the reception of Scripture, what man in his senses could proceed further than the first page of either Testament?

"Once more, you asked me to explain how this change could be effected—I will promise to tell you, if you will first explain to me how five loaves and three small fishes, after feeding five thousand persons, were more than would fill twelve baskets. Oh! Sir, indeed to be free of your Lord, I must tell you such reasoning is not of God. I may say so from the authority of Scripture, for it tells us, it is *by faith we must be saved*, and *faith is the evidence of things not seen*, whereas, you condemn me because I believe without being able to *see, feel, and taste.*

"My dear Sir, pardon me, but I must return your own words upon you, and remind you we shall all three have to account for what passed the morning I saw you. I now humble myself before God, and entreat He will give me grace to profit by what passed, and pardon all that I was deficient in. You, Sir, if you are a sincere man, will do the same; but I tremble when I think of how you deceived my parent, and of the account you will have to render for those words you uttered. Such words and such reasoning from a Protestant minister ought to have sounded as a trumpet in his ear, telling him all was not right, that he had been deceived,

and that he was reared to believe a lie. It
should at least have stirred him up to search,
and to arouse himself, for if such be the case,
the time is little enough to repair the error of
a whole life.   He is sincere: sir, I pray God,
so you may be; but for him I am as importun-
ate with God as ever Dives was to Abraham
for his five brethren.   I pray also for you, sir,
although faith that is not strong can hope
nothing for you, for as it is hard for a camel
to go through the eye of a needle, so hard is
it for a rich man, or one who derives his
riches from preaching a false faith, to be
converted. But with God nothing is impossible.
Faith is His especial gift, and I know full
well unless He bestow it, one would rise from
the dead in vain to produce it.   Christ said
Himself, ' no man can come unto Me unless
my Father draw him.'   Oh, then sir, if ever
it be your lot to be thus drawn, and I hope
it may, as you told me your own mother had
been a Catholic, and as she now, I trust,
pleads for you in heaven ; oh, forget not then
to undo by your testimony and your prayers
what you did that morning to keep my father
in the darkness of unbelief.   I commit you
both to God, who is merciful and just, and
remain most respectfully

" Your humble Servant,
"FANNY MARIA PITTAR."

To this letter I never received an answer. One would have thought this zealous man would have thought it worth his while to make one effort by way of reply to recover the sheep that had strayed; but no—a soul who could believe such an absurdity as that a part of a thing could ever become a whole, (as in the case of each host becoming a whole Christ), was not worth a thought. This was another of his arguments against our receiving Christ whole and entire in the sacrament. Oh folly, folly, such reasoning indeed should be sufficient to awake one out of their slumber, but alas! it is not. Fancy a reasonable mind on all other subjects being able to say, " My children, I wish you to be read and fully instructed on all subjects save one, and on that subject I command you never to hear or read a line—that subject the Catholic faith;" and fancy children arrived at the years of discretion satisfied, because a secret voice tells them that to examine into Catholicity they must embrace it. But I will forbear while I am in the land of prayer; I will pray and hope for the parent who issues the command, and for the sisters and brothers who quietly assented to it.

One word more, and then I conclude. To you who still condemn me, I would simply ask,—will you answer for my soul at the

great and final day of judgment, or think you
it will avail you should you hear the great
Judge declare I had saved my soul by becoming
a Catholic—think you, I say, it will avail
you to urge you thought I was wrong? No,
you know such an excuse will not avail you
then, and you also know you will not be
responsible for me ; therefore my word to
you is to take heed to yourselves.

But to those who may be more just and
reasonable, and who allow I had just cause
for this change, even to them, I leave my last
charge ; *search for yourselves*, for if I had
reason to change, so is there reason you
should do so also. See what this religion is,
that is so universally despised and abused,
and still has power, as with the strength of
iron, to hold and retain those who enrol themselves on its lists, and those firmest who once
were most clamorous against it. Search,
I say, for yourselves, and think not you overcome the truth when you commit it to the
flames ; no, if it meets no better defeat than
this, it is but consumed to rise up in judgment
against you.

Search, therefore, from the only source
you can depend upon. Would you condemn
a Protestant for his belief, on the testimony
of an infidel? No, you would not:—then
refuse not to Catholics what you would

demand for yourself. Go then to those to whom the Church's faith is confided, to her clergymen who are devoted to her interests, though other motives are charged upon them. Go to them, I say again, who have given up all for their Master's service. They are public property, the poor man's friend as well as the rich, and whose reward is to win souls into Christ's fold. Speak not ill of these men until you have been eye-witness to their evil deeds, and when you witness these, remember there was a Judas! Go, and may God only deal with you as graciously and as generously as He has with me, and give you but an equal share of joy and peace, and your soul will be more than satisfied—more than rewarded, for all it may have suffered in the trials unavoidable in changing any faith, be it what it may, for Catholicity.

FANNY MARIA PITTAR.

March, 1842.

APPENDIX.—A.

The Catholic Church has ever been accused of teaching the doctrine of Exclusive Salvation, but those who take the Scriptures for their guide and interpret them by private judgment forget that this doctrine is likewise taught by themselves. Let us examine briefly the doctrine of the Church.

All must acknowledge that there is but one God, but one faith, baptism, sheep-fold, and one Shepherd; and that if there are sheep out of this one fold, they are to be brought into the fold in order to be saved; "this is the ark," &c. Now here is the whole system, theoretical and practical, of Exclusive Salvation. It is the declaration of our Lord Himself, that His fold is one. Nor is it Christian nor just to try and distort His words and suit them to human notions. But it will be asked, "Are you so intolerant as to say that we shall be excluded from heaven?" Our answer must be, "We judge you not, we leave you individually to be weighed in the scales of eternal justice." Yet

truth assures us that there is but one fold.
And again, "God daily added to the Church
such as should be saved." What are we to
conclude? Can we look for salvation elsewhere? The only exception the Church
makes is in the case of invincible ignorance.

Let us briefly examine this very doctrine
held by those who take umbrage at the
teaching of the Church. Do they not exclude
from salvation those who disbelieve the
Trinity? Do they not read the exclusive
clauses of the Athanasian Creed? What do
they mean by the term Catholic Church?
Why baptize infants, and why speak of
heretics and schismatics? Why refuse Christian burial to the unbaptized, and to suicides?
Why send missionaries to convert Infidels,
Jews, Mahommedans? Why spend so many
millions in circulating the Bible? All this is
essential to salvation or it is not. If it is not
essential, why speak and act as if it were?
But if it is essential for salvation, then they
themselves fall under the charge of intolerance
and of teaching Exclusive Salvation.

We now adduce their own written testimony on this point.

1. Profession of the Kirk of Scotland,
Glasgow, 1771, article 16. "As we believe
in one God, so do we most constantly believe
that there hath been, now is, and to the end

shall be, one Kirk out of which Kirk neither *life* nor eternal *felicity* is to be hoped for nor had; and therefore we utterly abhor the *blasphemy* of those who affirm that men who live according to equity and justice shall be saved in whatever religion they have lived." This language needs no comment.

2. Her subsequent confession of faith agreed on by the Westminster Divines, approved by the General Assembly, and ratified by Parliament, holds the same language: " The visible Church, which is also Catholic or Universal, consists of all those throughout the whole world that profess the true Religion, and is the kingdom of the Lord, the house and family of God, out of which there is no *ordinary* possibility of salvation." This is strong enough.

3. The next Protestant authority is King James I. of England, 1612. He speaks through Isaac Casaubon, his agent, whom he rewarded for writing against the Catholics: "The King plainly believes without fallacy or deceit, that there is but *one* true Church called Catholic or universal, *out of which* he holds that no salvation is to be expected." Casaubon to Card. Perron, p. 10.

4. The Netherland Protestants, in their profession of faith, 1561, and approved by the famous synod of Dort, 1619, gives us the
10

following very express language: "We believe and confess *one only* Catholic and universal Church; it will continue till time shall be no more." Confessio Belgica, art. 27.

Again, art. 28, p. 141, they say: "Now this society and congregation is the society of those who are to be saved, and *there is no salvation out of it.*"

5. In the French Protestant Catechism the minister asks the child: "Why is the article of the Creed, respecting the forgiveness of sin, placed next after Catholic Church, communion of Saints?" The answer is: "Because *no one* obtains pardon of his sins who is not incorporated with the people of God and the unity of the Church." Minister: "So then my child, out of the Church there is nothing but death and damnation? A. Without doubt; for those who separate and form a sect apart, can never expect salvation whilst they so continue." Amsterdam Edition 1710, p. 283.

6. Let us now hear Martin Luther, the chief of so-called Reformers: "I know some," he says, " were of opinion fifteen years ago that every man would be saved in his own way of thinking. Now what is this but to collect all the enemies of Christ into one body? Nay, in such case, there must have been no need of Christ and His Gospel *at all.*

Strange then must be the impudence of the Zuinglians to have not only broached such a doctrine themselves, but to palm it on me." Luth. in 47, Gen. tom. 6, p. 633.

7. 'Tillotson, tom. 6, p. 245, Edit. post. obit. says, "If the Church of Rome be the Catholic Church, it is *necessary* to be of that communion, because *out of the* Catholic Church there is no ordinary possibility of salvation."

8. Dr. Pearson, on the Creed, p. 349, Edit. 1669, has the following words: " The necessity of believing the Catholic Church appears in this, that Christ has appointed it as the only way to eternal life. Christ never appointed *two ways to heaven*, nor did He build a Church to save *some*, and make another institution for other *men's salvation.* ' There is no other name under heaven whereby we must be saved, but the name of Jesus; and that name is not otherwise given than in the Church.'

"As *none* were saved from the deluge but such as were in the ark of Noah, so *none will ever* escape the eternal wrath of God which belong not to the Church of God."

Now after this evidence to accuse Catholics of intolerance and want of charity on this point, will be not only unreasonable, but as Dr. Tillotson phrases it, "dint of imprudence and facing down of mankind."

APPENDIX.—B.

The error of the Predestinarian is not perhaps as old as many more which gave their advocates unenviable notoriety in the Christian world. Until the 16th century, this error had but few conspicuous advocates. Calvin and Beza taught that Almighty God had so predestined every one whom He called, that, once *elected*, they could not lose the grace which He gave them, so that whether they sinned or did not sin, a glorious inheritance awaited them. This doctrine would certainly be pleasing to flesh and blood. The Pelagians and Semi-Pelagians fell into a similar error.

Born in Holland in 1560, Arminius, educated partly at the University of Leyden and partly at Geneva, undertook to defend the error of Predestination. In studying the arguments, however, he fell into sentiments very contrary to those he had undertaken to confute. First he could not understand, as Beza and Calvin taught, how the Father of all could pre-destine men to eternal damnation. It would be against the mercy of God, making Him the Author of sin, and destroying the liberty and free-will of man.

Gomar, professor of theology at Leyden, espoused the cause of the Predestinarians, and the two parties filled the United States with tumult and disorder. Now it is quite clear that all these teachers rejected an infallible authority, whose business it was to fix the Religious Creed of Christians. Amongst themselves there was no bond of union in any way. They lived in a continual antagonism to one another.

Luther also on his side taught that all human actions were sins, and still insisted that a man justified by faith could never sin at all; because, according to him, God will not impute sin to any one thus justified. Moreover, he rejects free will, which he calls a slave, and says that God operates in man both sin and virtue equally! Now all the errors of those teachers spring from the same source—the erroneous principle of Private Judgment. This is the principle by which they sought to overthrow the authority of the Church, and free themselves from the obedience of faith.

The Catholic Church invariably taught that the understanding as well as the heart of man was to be made subject to the yoke of Christ. *Faith*, as St. Paul teaches, was *to make captive every understanding* to its teaching. She teaches that every soul is predestined or known to God from all eternity—the good and the bad. This fore-knowledge does not take away the free will of man, nor lessen his liberty. Even as the angels who rebelled were free to serve or not serve, so is man free to submit his understanding and his will, or not submit them. Upon this act depends his own fate : *" Many are called, few are chosen ;"* the few are those who use grace, the many are those who abuse the grace which God in His mercy freely offers without any previous merit on their part, " He rejects the proud because of their pride, which opposes Him. He gives grace to the humble, because they are *not proud* and do not resist Him." By this teaching the apparent difficulty is resolved of reconciling the will of God with the free will of man. " God wills that all men should come to the knowledge of the truth." But the majority of men will the contrary, and prefer darkness to light, and hence it is said : " They are reprobate, though they could have been of the elect," by co-operating with the grace given them: in other words, by bowing down the understanding as well as the heart, and taking care to hear " the Church," whose mission it is to teach all truth, whilst it is the duty of all men to receive it : " He that believeth not shall be condemned."

APPENDIX.—C.

In separating from the Church and refusing to abide by her authority, we find every heresiarch and his followers took refuge in the Scriptures, interpreted according to each one's own sense or understanding.

This was a natural act on their part, for, leaving the Church, they took with them the Scriptures to justify or at least to give colour of orthodoxy to schism. The Scriptures of the Old Testament are useful as teaching much and as foreshadowing the New Covenant, the Law of grace and truth. Hence all Christians may claim a right to prove from them the truth of Christianity or the New Law. The New Testament, however, is the book of the Church, and hence, united with the Old Testament, is called the Bible or the Book, which latter it signifies being a Greek word. To hold the Book, however, and to understand it or explain its sense to others, is quite a different thing. The Book was the property of the Church, it was the volume of her authority, containing most of her doctrines or the germ of nearly all, and the history also of Infant Christianity, or the foundation of our Lord's kingdom. To separate from the com-

munion of the Church is the crime of schism.
To set up another society calling itself a
Church, and to teach doctrines at variance
with those of the Church, is heresy and schism.
To separate from the Church, and then to
usurp her authority and her mission, and to
use her Book against herself and in favour of
error, is an impiety which needs hardly even a
shadow of proof. The rule of faith is the
voice of the Church teaching divine truth as
revealed to her, and delivered to her care as a
precious deposit by God. To guard this
deposit from error, the Spirit of Truth was
given her. The Scriptures have emanated
from her; it is from her the heretic and the
schismatic, once her own children, received
the Scriptures. In latter times, especially,
they have taken upon themselves not only to
interpret its difficulties and obscure passages,
and to give its deep and mysterious sense to
the world, but they have also undertaken the
task of fixing the canon of the Scriptures, or
of deciding the books that are inspired and the
books not inspired. And having thus arrogated
to themselves the work of God's Church, they
have wound up by declaring that the Scriptures so approved by themselves are their only
rule of faith.

As a farther proof of the absurdity of this
doctrine, every one is left to take the sense of

this rule according to his private understanding or judgment. "To hear the Church," our Lord's precept is thus violated, the judgment of the Church is rejected, and the unanimous voice of antiquity speaks in vain. Supposing the Church were to grant that this principle was not dangerous, she would at least urge the dilemma as follows:—Either your rule of faith is all Scripture, or only a part of it. If your only rule of faith is all Scripture, how do you know that in your present Bible you have all the Scriptures that were written?

Where is the *Book of the Wars?* mentioned in Numbers xxi. 14?

Or the Book of 'the Righteous or Just?— Josua x. 13; II. Kings i. 18.

Or the Acts of King David? 1 Chronicles xxix. 29.

Or the Book of Samuel the Seer? Chron.

Or that of Nathan the Prophet? Chron.

Or of Gad the Seer? Chron.

Where are all the Acts of Solomon?— 2 Chron. ix. 29.

Or the Prophecy of Ahijas? Chron.

Or the Visions of Addo the Seer? Chron.

Where are the Acts of Josaphat? Chron. xx. 34.

Or the Book of Jehu, the son of Hanani? Chron. xx. 34.

Where are the remainder of Solomon's 3000 parables, and 1005 poems? 3 Kings iv. 32.

Where are all the other Chronicles of the kings of Juda and Israel, to which references are made in the Books of Kings?

Where are the treatises on plants and animals, written by Solomon? 3 Kings iv. 33.

Now we come to the New Testament. The last lines of St. John's Gospel declare that the words and acts of our Lord, if they were *all* written, the world itself would not contain the books.

The Gospel narratives therefore are not complete.

We next come to the Apostles. St. Paul 1 Cor. v. 9, says: "I wrote unto you in an Epistle, not to keep company with," &c.

Writing to the Colossians, iv. 16, he commands them to read his epistle to the Laodiceans.

Where are the above Epistles? Here also we may add: St. Matthew says in his Gospel, xxvii. 9: "Then was fulfilled that which was spoken by the Prophet Jeremiah, saying: 'And they took the thirty pieces of silver, the price of Him that was set at a price by the children of Israel.'" Where can this important passage be found?

St. Matthew, ii. 23, writes: "It was spoken by the Prophets that Christ should be called a

Nazarene !" Where in the books of prophecy are these words to be found?

The learned Dr. Lawrence, Protestant Archbishop of Cashel in Ireland, in his Dissertation on the Book of Henoch, doubts not this book to be authentic. It is said to have been found in the last century by Bruce the traveller in Abyssinia, and is now translated into English, and printed in London in 1833.

This book is corroborated by St. Jude the Apostle, in his Epistle, ver. 14, "Of these Henoch also, the seventh from Adam, prophecied saying: 'Behold the Lord cometh with thousands of His saints.'" According to this testimony, the above Scriptures are lost. What we have therefore received from the Church is only a part, or at least is not the whole of the Scriptures of the Old and New Testament. How to get out of this dilemma seems very hard, yet we believe human ingenuity does and will ever contrive to surmount the most reasonable obstacles. A very learned and ingenious Bishop of the Established Church in these kingdoms, cooly asserted that there were no such things as human bodies in reality. A very convenient doctrine this would be, especially if we could dispense with all their necessities.

PRINTED BY RICHARDSON AND SON, DERBY.